ACKNOWLEDGEMENTS

CW01500904

I wouldn't be able to write any of these books without the help of a multitude of people who have assisted along the way. Specifically, I would like to thank my editors, David Gilmore and Randy Olsen, and my team of proof readers—without whom, you would be receiving a by far inferior version of the book you read today—JC Barb, Rohen Kapur, Mike Riley, Kris Densley, Mykel Densley, Liia Miller, Peter Gifford, Ross Jarratt, Forest Olivier, and my mother, Susan Cartwright.

For technical help with regards to modern aviation, I would like to thank Chris Chmiel from the Australian RAAF who spent hours trying to explain the intricate ins and outs of a modern jetliner from the point of view of the pilot.

As always, all mistakes reside squarely on my shoulders.

Christopher Cartwright

CHRISTOPHER CARTWRIGHT

THE PHEONIX SANCTION

A SAM REILLY NOVEL

PROLOGUE

Please note that I know the hazards. I want to do it. Because I want to try. As men have tried. Women must too. And when they fail, their failure must be of a challenge to others.

–Amelia Earhart's letter to her husband on the eve of her last flight.

Lae Airfield, Papua New Guinea–July 2, 1937

I T WAS 10 A.M. LOCAL TIME when the heavily loaded Lockheed Model 10 Electra stopped at the end of the grass field. The American twin-engine, all-metal monoplane, with its unique double tail and twin rudder system looked decidedly futuristic, a jarring contrast against the harsh backdrop of the hot Papua New Guinea jungle.

Amelia Earhart met her navigator Fred Noonan's eye with a broad grin. "You ready to make history?"

He made a curt nod. "Good to go."

Amelia pushed the twin throttles to full. All nine cylinders of each of the Pratt and Whitney R-1340-S3H1 Wasp engines sputtered into life, their pitch rising to a gravelly roar, sending all 600 horsepower to the twin propellers. The 9 foot, 7/8-inch, two-bladed, Hamilton Standard variable-pitch, constant-speed propellers spun faster until they disappeared into an invisible whir.

She glanced at the gauges. The engine RPM registered 2,250 for each engine. Amelia made a broad and relaxed smile. Despite what people might think she was doing with what some called the stunt of circumnavigation, the simple fact was, she loved the adventure of flight.

She took a deep breath in. The edge of her lips opened in a grin, revealing large and evenly spaced, white teeth, except for a noticeable gap between her two front teeth. "Here we go!"

Loaded with 1151 US gallons of 100 percent high octane gasoline, the Electra crept forward. She gained speed slowly, like a long-distance runner, not a sprinter; she lazily picked up her pace. Two thirds of the way down the runway, Amelia felt the gentle buffeting of the wheel, teasing and begging her to be released.

She applied firm downward pressure.

Back in March, the overburdened Electra had suffered an uncontrolled ground loop during takeoff from Hawaii, causing the forward landing gear to collapse and both propellers to hit the ground as the plane skidded on its belly. Surprisingly, no one was badly injured, but it meant her first round-the-world flight had been a failure, and the Electra needed to be sent back stateside for significant repairs.

No. She wouldn't make that mistake again.

Her eyes darted toward the Air Speed Indicator.

It crept up to the minimum take-off speed. She held the wheel firmly for another few precious seconds and then gently pulled the wheel toward her chest.

Released from its earthly restraints, the Electra climbed at a conservative rate of 550 feet per minute, just shy of half its potential maximum climb rate of 1,000 feet per minute.

Her focus turned briefly over her right shoulder, and her eyes swept the remains of the Lae Jungle below. "Good bye, Papua New Guinea. Next stop, Howland Island."

The name Electra came from a star in the cluster of the Pleiades.

It was among the nearest star clusters to Earth and the cluster most obvious to the naked eye in the night sky, and as such, the nine brightest stars of the Pleiades are named for the Seven Sisters of Greek mythology: Sterope, Merope, Electra, Maia, Taygeta, Celaeno, and Alcyone, along with their parents Atlas and Pleione. As daughters of Atlas, the Hyades were sisters of the Pleiades.

The Electra was 38 feet, 7 inches long with a wingspan of 55 feet and an overall height of 10 feet, 1 inch — all in total a speck on the vastness of the Pacific Ocean as it made its way across the 2,556 statute miles between Lae Airfield and Howland Island.

The shortest route was known as the Great Circle, which basically formed a straight line from Lae to Howland Island over the curvature of the Earth. But, as they approached New Britain Island, less than four hours into their journey, large rain squalls to the east forced them to divert to the south of the island, around Gasmata. The cloud cover came in thick and Amelia took the aircraft from 7,000 feet up to 10,000 feet to climb above it.

Fred Noonan unclipped his harness and stood up. "I'd better get you a new course."

"Please do," Amelia replied, her voice curt, but not unhappy. "I'll try to keep us above the cloud long enough for you to take a reading."

Noonan was tall, very thin, with dark auburn-hair. His cobalt blue eyes were large and liquid. At forty-three years of age, he walked with a determined stride as he passed the four auxiliary fuel tanks in the passenger compartment, heading aft along the fuselage to reach his navigation station.

Passenger windows had been eliminated throughout the

entire passenger section of the fuselage, with the exception of two rectangular, distortion free windows on either side of the navigator's table. He took out his sextant, marked the time, and took a reading while Amelia attempted to keep the Electra as steady as possible.

He made his notes on the navigation chart fixed to the table and then plotted a new course. His gaze traced its way along the new course, past Nauru, through the Gilbert Islands — a chain of sixteen tiny atolls — before finally coming to rest on Howland Island.

Noonan calculated the distance between the Gilbert Islands and Howland Island as 1,152 miles. If they got into trouble locating Howland, there was always the possibility of flying a reciprocal course. The islands were mostly uninhabited, but he was certain they could land on a beach. Worst case scenario, they could always ditch in the coastal waters and swim to shore — not that it would ever come to that. They had provisions for enough fuel to reach the Gilberts if they had to.

Navigation to the untrained seemed like witchcraft in medieval times, but it was very much based on science and exact calculations. Mistakes could be made certainly, but those risks could be mitigated with knowledge and understanding. Solid mathematics, an accurate time piece, good maps, and due diligence made it safe.

He had vast experience in both marine and flight navigation. His original training was in the merchant navy, in which he continued working on merchant ships throughout World War I. Serving as an officer on ammunition ships, his harrowing wartime service included being on three vessels that were sunk from under him by German U-boats. He went on to become a naval captain and a flight navigator, who had recently left Pan Am, after establishing most of the company's China Clipper seaplane routes across the Pacific. In addition to more modern navigational tools, Noonan, as a licensed sea captain, was known for carrying a ship's sextant on these flights.

He gave Amelia the new compass bearing, and he felt the Electra gently bank to its left on that course. Afterward, he set about performing a series of routine maintenance checks on the engines and instruments.

The flight continued through the night, crossing the International Date Line into yesterday morning. Noonan slept intermittently throughout the last third of the trip, before being awakened by Amelia.

She was whistling into the radio mic. It was a constant, chirping sound rather than any specific tone. It continued for some time. There was something strangely eerie about the whistle, despite its cheerful tone—a foreboding tease of dire times to come.

Noonan sat up, blinking, feeling his heart start to quicken.

"We've got a problem," Amelia said, her voice curt, but not harried. "You had better come up here."

Noonan checked his timepiece. It was nearly 6:20 a.m. in the local time zone. He'd overslept. Without preamble, he made his way to the cockpit. His eyes darted toward the dense cloud cover below and Amelia's carefree face. "I see you haven't managed to shake the cloud cover."

"No," she replied, meeting his gaze directly, her teeth lightly biting her bottom lip. "But that's not our only problem."

Noonan sat down in the copilot's seat. "What have we got?"

"I've been picking up a transmission from *Itasca* on 7500 kHz, but our radio detection frequency equipment was unable to determine a minimum frequency."

"Thus, you're not able to get a bearing on the *Itasca*."

"Exactly." She sighed. "I've been trying to get someone on Howland to take a navigational bearing on our transmission on 3105 kilocycles so they can give us a bearing."

"And?"

Amelia's face scrunched up slightly. "I'm having one hell of a time trying to establish two-way radio communications with the *US Coast Guard Cutter, Itasca*."

He glanced at the radio through an arched eyebrow. "How long have you been trying?"

"Nearly an hour."

"They might have switched early to the daytime frequency of 6210 kilocycles."

"They haven't. I've already tried to reach them on it."

Noonan relaxed into his seat, his hands folded neatly across his lap. Any problem worth solving required time, focus, and calm patience. Science could overcome any problem they were facing. "Have you heard from the *Itasca* at all in the last hour?"

Amelia nodded. "Yeah, multiple times, but they're clearly not receiving my messages."

Noonan thought about that for a moment. His eyes widened and he gasped, "Good God…"

Amelia finished it for him, "The two frequencies have started to bleed into each other!"

He knew exactly what was happening and just hoped they still had time to make a correction. Their radio worked on two frequencies, known as harmonic frequencies — 6210 and 3105. At certain hours of the day the two frequencies bled into one another.

It was a significant failing in his planning as navigator. It meant that they would be arriving at Howland Island at 8 a.m. during a time when the night time frequency of 3105 KCs was fading and 6210 would be bleeding in to take its place. Right now, they were in limbo — 3105 hadn't faded and 6210 wasn't on line — thus the *USCGC Itasca* and the *Electra* were only capable of intermittently receiving each other's messages.

Fred made a couple quick calculations with his pencil on the navigation chart Amelia had been using to keep track of their progress based on dead reckoning. She had made two more entries since he'd fallen asleep a couple hours earlier. One indicated increasing speed to 180 knots from 150 with a tail wind. He took it into account.

Fred unclipped his harness. "We're approximately a hundred and five miles out from Howland. Keep on this bearing. I'd better go take a reading. With goniometry out, we're on our own."

Amelia made a slight shrug of her shoulders. "We've made it this far on our own, no reason to think we can't reach Howland Island."

Noonan headed back, without mentioning that Howland Island was a flat sliver of land 6,500 feet long, 1,600 feet wide, and no more than 20 feet above the ocean waves. The island would be hard to distinguish from the similar looking cloud shapes.

By 7:30 a.m. local time, he had established just one bearing — the sun — which produced their longitude only. The cloud cover prohibited him from determining a ground bearing. Without a line of position, it was impossible to measure latitude. It required two bearings to establish a fix, and he only had one.

Noonan placed the folded navigation chart in front of Amelia. "We're somewhere here, along the sun line of 157/337."

Amelia ran her pale gray eyes across the penciled line. Her eyebrows arched. It clearly bisected Howland Island. She shook her head. "We're right on it. The question is do we fly northeast or southwest to reach it?"

Noonan didn't hesitate. "Southwest."

Her eyes narrowed. "Why?"

"It's a fifty-fifty chance either way."

"You don't have a hunch whether we drifted north or south of your original plotted course?"

Noonan spread his hands out. "No. I was right on track."

Her lips formed a hard line. "What makes you so certain we should fly southwest?"

"Because if I'm wrong and we fly northeast there's more than a thousand miles of open ocean, but if I'm wrong and we fly southeast, we're bound to hit the Phoenix Islands."

She tilted the wheel until the Electra banked to the right. "Southwest it is."

They both knew the Phoenix Islands were a group of eight unoccupied atolls and two submerged coral reefs some four hundred miles to the southeast of Howland Island. It would be a stretch, but he was reasonably confident they had the fuel to reach it.

Amelia descended below the cloud cover and depressed the mic. "USCGC *Itasca*. We must be on you but cannot see you. But gas is running low. Been unable to reach you by radio. We are flying at altitude 1,000 feet."

There was nothing but silence on the radio.

At 8:43 a.m. Amelia made her final attempt to achieve two-way radio communication with the *Itasca*. "We are on the line 157–337. Will repeat message. We will repeat this on 6210 kilocycles... We are running north and south on line, listening 6210."

There was nothing but silence.

Noonan sighed heavily. "I guess that's it then. We're on our own."

"Looks like it." Amelia tilted her head slightly and met his gaze directly. "Do you think we made the wrong choice?"

He cocked an eyebrow. "Are you asking whether or not I think we should have turned northeast instead of southeast?"

She nodded. "Yeah."

"No. Right or wrong we made the only choice available to us at the time. It's still the only choice available to us. We're committed now. No chance to set a reciprocal course and retrace our flight. If we're north of Howland we'll hit it on our way along this sunline. If we were southeast of Howland, then we definitely have enough fuel to reach the Phoenix Islands — either way, we're going to reach land."

Amelia laughed at his confidence. "I knew there was a reason

I brought you along. Thank you."

"You're welcome." He opened his mouth to speak, closed it again, and then said, "For what it's worth, I also believe in your flying ability to put us down safely on some beach somewhere once we reach land."

She expelled a deep breath of air. "It's a deal."

The Electra continued to fly on across the vastness of the ocean.

There was nothing visible but the sea. No land, no ships, no birds. No sign of the *Itasca's* smoke stack, whose boilers had been fed oil to produce a thick cloud of black smoke extending more than 200 feet into the air. Nothing heard on the radio. Only the drone of the engines, monotonously beating the propellers against the air at 1,000 feet.

With a quiet resolve, Noonan said, "I'll go prepare the life raft."

Amelia shook her head and grinned. "Not just yet. I think I see something up ahead."

Noonan squinted his eyes. All he could see was the eternal sea all the way to the horizon, where a tiny sliver of blue turned white. "I don't see anything."

Amelia pointed toward the horizontal line on the horizon. "That's whitewater up ahead!"

"My God, you're right!" He took a deep breath in. "That means there's a reef! And the only reef in this region is part of the Phoenix Islands!"

Amelia flew a clockwise circuit around the island, searching for a suitable landing site. The island was roughly 5 miles long by 1.5 miles wide and appeared uninhabited, or at least, their flyover didn't elicit any persons from the dense forest. The island itself was shaped like a somewhat elongated, triangular coral atoll with profuse vegetation and a large central marine lagoon of striking turquoise, dark blues, and opaline.

If need be, they could always land on the shallow lagoon and then swim to shore. It might prove to be the safest option, given the danger of landing near the breaking reef.

At the end of the circuit, Noonan spotted the intact remains of a large shipwreck on the reef to the northwest side of the island. There, the broad shelf running out to the reef edge had little to no water on it.

Noonan met her eye. "Are you planning on staying up here all day?"

"You're right, that's as good a landing spot as we're ever going to get."

She brought the Electra down, setting up for a low-level circuit, flying past the whitewash in the downwind run in a counterclockwise direction. In the process, they both studied the reef. It was dry and years of constant waves had smoothed it to a perfect landing strip.

Amelia pulled on the landing gear lever, followed by the flaps. "Landing gear down. Flaps fully extended."

Noonan looked at her. His jaw set firm. "You know, if you pull this off, there's still time for the *Itasca* to locate us. Then we'll get refueled, and we might just be in Honolulu by the end of the week."

She smiled. "You bet we can!"

Amelia set the fuel mixture to full rich and the propellers to high RPM as she banked onto their final approach.

She pulled the twin throttles back to idle.

The Electra glided gently toward the landing site.

Noonan gripped the side of the cockpit for support. Their lives depended on the outcome of the next thirty seconds. His heart raced and he found himself unintentionally holding his breath.

Amelia pulled the wheel toward her chest causing the Electra to flare. A moment later, the wheels touched down on the smooth reef.

She applied the brakes and the Electra came to a complete

stop. She shut off the fuel mix, and the engine sputtered and conked out, leaving them in the silence of the distant waves.

Noonan hugged her. "Well done!"

"It's not Howland Island, but it will do," Amelia replied, her eyes wide and her relaxed face filled with teasing. "Now, you had better work out just where we are."

Amelia Earhart climbed out of the Electra.

A crepuscular ray pierced the cloud overhead, turning the dark water of the reef to emerald. She breathed in the warm air. At 10:32 a.m. the tropical air was already racing toward 100 degrees Fahrenheit.

At 5 feet 8 inches, she had a lanky build and proportionate features. She squatted down and climbed beneath the wing. Her blonde hair, which she kept short for convenience, blew in the endless westerly sea breeze. She ducked down under the fuselage, running her hands along the landing gear. She took her hands back and glanced at them. They were clean. The struts were intact and there was no leaking oil.

She stepped out the opposite side and stared at the aircraft.

Her gaze traced the wings and propellers, across to the nose of the Electra as she circled around, before finally settling on the twin tails and rudder mechanism — everything was intact.

Amelia's cheeks dimpled as her lips formed a wide grin.

Noonan met her eye. "Well, Amelia... what do you think? Will she fly?"

"You bet she will." Amelia picked up a smooth rock from the beach and skimmed it across the shallow water of the inside reef. Turning to face him directly, she asked, "Any idea where she's going to fly from?"

"No. But I do know something."

"What?"

"If she's ever going to fly again, it will need to be within the next week."

Her eyes narrowed. "Why?"

"I have the tide charts for the Phoenix Islands."

"And?"

"They show it's currently a neap tide."

She arched her trim eyebrow. "Meaning?"

"It's the lowest point in the multi-day tidal cycle." Noonan sighed heavily. "There's no water on the broad shelf running to the outer reef, but there will be. Just have a look at the previous watermarks."

"Are you telling me, after all this, the damned tide is going to come in and steal the Electra from us?"

Noonan squinted, running his eyes across the waves breaking across the distant reef. "In time. But by now the *Itasca* will have initiated a search and rescue. If I know your husband, already damn near half the fleet stationed at Honolulu will be on their way south to help. They'll stay nearby Howland at first, but soon enough, someone will make the obvious connection and follow the 157–337 sunline, taking them straight to us. The question is how long it will take them to reach that conclusion?"

Amelia smiled and started walking to the end of the reef where the beach reached the jungle. "One way or another, we'd better make sure we're out of here by that time."

"Where are you going?"

"To get out of this damned heat. Come on, let's see what this island offers in terms of food and water."

"I'll stay here and see if I can get the radio to work."

Amelia ran the palms of her hands through her hair, wiping away the perspiration that was already beading up on her forehead. She met his gaze and shook her head. "Not now. We'll need to conserve our energy and water supply. It's too hot out here in the direct sun. Besides, we'll need to start the engines to power the radio. We'll try again tonight."

CHRISTOPHER CARTWRIGHT I **13**

"Agreed."

It became quickly apparent that the island on which they had become castaways was far from the dreamy islands of Robinson Crusoe.

The desert atoll had no fresh water and temperatures which exceeded 100 degrees Fahrenheit in the shade. The island was like many of those Amelia and Noonan had seen throughout the Pacific, wooded in indigenous forest dominated by the Buka, a large tropical softwood tree, feral coconut, and shrubs known as Scaevola frutescens — which made it hard to penetrate let alone search for food and water.

Tired and weary, they took turns to rest throughout the heat of the day. By early afternoon, they split up and searched the outskirts of the island. Along the northwestern reef laid the remains of a large freighter that appeared to have run aground. A nameplate, still visible, gave the name SS *Norwich City*. The internal hull had been savaged by fire while the exterior had been bombarded by the sea, leaving nothing of value.

They returned a couple hours later to the Electra. Noonan reported that he'd made it to the southern tip of the reef, and that he'd discovered a small trail leading into the dense forest of the island about midway. He'd followed the trail and found that it ended shortly at the saltwater lagoon that encompassed the interior of the atoll.

They agreed to search the island's interior in the morning.

In the cool of the night, Amelia started the engines and attempted to use the HF radio to call for help. After failing to receive any response after fifteen minutes, she killed the engine and went to sleep.

In the morning she woke up in the gray of predawn. Noonan was already awake, staring out at the ocean.

She said, "Good morning."

"Morning."

"Shall we make an early start of it?"

"Yes. We'd better. What if someone comes by?"

Amelia glanced at the remains of the nearby shipwreck. "If anyone does a flyover they're bound to spot the Electra."

"What makes you so sure?"

"The wreck of the *SS Norwich City*. It's an obvious scar on the otherwise untainted reef. It was the first thing I spotted at a thousand feet. Anyone flying overhead would spot it, and a second later, their eyes would recognize the Electra on the reef next to it."

"Good thinking."

She smiled. "I'd like to say I thought that far ahead, but it was just luck. I only realized when I looked back at the two stranded vessels from the shore."

"What if the *Itasca* sends a search party?"

"What if?"

"We'll be gone all day."

"They'll wait for us. Just in case, I left a note in the cockpit to say that we'd gone to explore the southeastern end of the island."

"All right. I see you've thought of everything. Let's go."

They followed the trail Noonan had taken the previous afternoon to the atoll's lagoon. The ground was flat and porous, leaving no freshwater for their consumption. There were enough supplies on board the Electra to keep them alive for about a week, but they wouldn't make it much longer than that.

At the lagoon, Amelia spotted something dark hidden in the underbrush of the dense forest in the southwestern region. "What is that?"

Noonan stared at the place where she was pointing. "I don't know. It could be an old hut."

"Let's go find out."

They followed the outskirts of the lagoon in a counterclockwise direction until they reached the southern end, where the shallow water of the lagoon ended in a long white stretch of sand. Where the lagoon met the forest was a thick rockery of black pumice.

Amelia stopped.

Noonan asked, "What?"

"Let's make an SOS sign here on the white sand. With the black stones on the white sand this will stand out like a giant signpost."

Noonan shrugged. "Okay, let's double up on our chances."

They worked until midday to lay the black pumice stones side by side to form the letters SOS in thirty feet high lettering. Afterward, they rested beneath the shade of a forest of coconut trees, carefully drinking small amounts of their precious water.

When the worst of the heat had subsided, they continued following the lagoon until it reached a decidedly man-made waterway leading into the forest. At a glance, Amelia knew someone had intentionally carved a path into the jungle for the waterway.

They stepped into the warm water, following it beneath the thick vegetation. The water was shallow, no more than a foot deep, and roughly six wide.

Sixty feet into the makeshift canal, they both stopped.

There, in front of them was a large shed with a tin roof. The canal entered the storage facility and inside were hundreds of drums of aviation fuel.

"What is this place?" Amelia asked.

"It looks like a fuel depot," Noonan replied, pointing out the obvious. "It looks like someone's been using the lagoon as a landing site and refueling station for seaplanes."

Amelia glanced at the tin roof, painted in greens and yellows to form a tropical camouflage. "Someone's gone to a lot of trouble to heavily conceal this place from the air."

"It would seem so. The question is, why?"

Amelia looked at the side of the first drum of aviation fuel. Oriental writing that she couldn't decipher lined the edge of it. "What is this writing, Chinese?"

Noonan shook his head. "Japanese."

She stared at the depot through narrowed eyes. "Why would the Japanese be storing hundreds of drums of aviation fuel in secret out here?"

"There's only one reason I can think of."

"What's that?"

Noonan swallowed. "In prelude to war."

Over the course of the next five days, Amelia and Noonan split their time and effort between shifting the 55-gallon drums of aviation fuel, foraging for food, and using the HF radio to try and contact someone for help in the night time. They subsisted on a diet of coconut crabs, turtles, giant clams, and birds. There was no fresh water on the island, which meant they needed to ration their water supply from the Electra to last until they could refuel and takeoff again.

They needed twenty drums to fill the Electra's 1,100-gallon long range fuel tanks. That meant twenty individual trips of nearly three miles. A single trip entailed floating a drum along the shallow canal and around the shallow edge of the lagoon, before rolling it across the trail to the western beach and then along nearly two miles of sand.

Amelia imagined the world's reaction when they flew into Honolulu more than a week after going missing. It would be the story of the century. The triumph of good over adversity, a tale of tenacity beating despondency, as two castaways saved themselves. It was a good thought, and she found herself cheerful on her way back to the fuel depot for the 17th drum.

She headed down the southern end of the lagoon and stopped — because the black pumice stones that she and Noonan had so painstakingly lined up in the shape of SOS, were now missing!

Noonan met her gaze, his face filled with a fear she'd never seen him wear.

From out of the jungle on the opposite side of the lagoon, a Japanese soldier kneeled down and aimed a rifle at them.

Noonan shouted, "Run!"

Amelia turned.

A shot fired, followed by others in rapid succession until the rifle's magazine was empty.

She dropped to the ground. Looking over her right shoulder, and saw Noonan covered in blood, breathing heavily.

"Sweet Jesus!" she cried.

Noonan tried to speak, but only frothy blood came from his mouth.

Amelia turned to help him, grabbing his hand and squeezing it hard.

Another shot fired.

It went wide over their heads.

Noonan swallowed, gritted his teeth, trying to muster the energy to speak. "Go!"

"I'm not leaving you!"

He met her eye, his voice emphatic, "Yes, you are!"

She shook her head. "I can drag you back to the Electra!"

"No. You can't!" His cobalt blue eyes turned to steel and defiance. "You have to escape. Someone needs to tell the world, the Japanese are preparing for an invasion."

Amelia mouthed the words, "No, I won't leave you," but already, she knew Noonan was speaking the truth. Their lives didn't matter. If she was injured, she would have insisted on him leaving her behind.

"Go!" Turning to the practicalities of her escape, Noonan said, "Don't fly to Honolulu. You'll never reach it with your current fuel supply."

"Where should I go?"

"Set a bearing southeast, to New Zealand!"

Amelia looked at him through tear-filled eyes, squeezed his hand, and said, "I won't let the world forget what you have done!"

She then turned and ran.

Amelia didn't stop running until she reached the Electra. She removed the wheel chock and climbed onboard, closing the hatch behind her.

She flicked on the master switch and started the engines, quickly advancing the throttles forward until the propellers picked up their speed, disappearing in a whir.

Amelia reduced power to the starboard engine and increased throttle to the port engine, causing the aircraft to rotate on the spot. She brought the Electra to a full stop facing south. Far in the distance, she spotted something that turned her blood to ice.

A man was running toward her.

And he was carrying a rifle!

Amelia pushed both throttles as far forward as she could. The Electra pulled forward, as though eager to finally escape the confines of the castaway island.

Up ahead, the soldier took aim at her.

She glanced at the Air Speed Indicator. It read, 85 miles per hour. Not nearly enough for takeoff.

A shot fired.

She ducked instinctively, but she didn't need to. The Electra would take off in a nose-up position, meaning that the metallic nose of the aircraft and part of the fuselage would be between her and the man firing at her.

Her attacker might still get lucky and damage an important part of the Electra, but it was unlikely he would be able to stop her taking off.

She glanced at the Air Speed Indicator. It now read 120 miles per hour.

Amelia held the wheel forward for the count of three more seconds, and then pulled it gently to her chest.

She heard the staccato of multiple shots being fired.

A hundred feet in the air, she banked to the left, and set a course southeast — toward New Zealand.

Amelia flew on into the night and into the next day.

As the Electra flew on, reaching into her 20th hour, Amelia felt the tingling grip of Death pawing at the back of her neck.

Had she missed New Zealand altogether?

She had already flicked over to the final reserve fuel tank, but even those, too, were now almost completely dry.

The twin propellers continued to beat the air.

The left engine went first.

For a total of three minutes the right one continued, before it misfired, sputtered, and eventually conked out completely.

Amelia pushed the wheel forward, dipping the nose, avoiding an immediate stall, before settling into the Electra's optimum glide ratio.

At five thousand feet, there was still time.

Her eyes raked the sea for any sign of land.

Failing that, she studied the swell, trying to determine the best place to put down on the sea. Her gaze caught something that didn't quite seem right. The large swell was flowing in a southeasterly direction and then flattened out into a millpond. The sea changed from the monotonous midnight blue of deep, dark ocean water, into shades of cyan, pale azure, and aquamarine.

She was over shallow water.

That didn't make sense. Even off course, anywhere near New Zealand was surrounded by deep water.

The question remained, where was she?

Far into the distance, the water turned a deep blue, nearing shades of black.

Amelia squinted her eyes trying to get a better grasp on what she was seeing. She corrected her course, just slightly to the south, aiming for the anomaly.

The Electra glided on dutifully and as she approached the site, Amelia realized for the first time that she was looking at the back of a small mountainous atoll. The black, glassy volcanic stone formed the shape of a large half-dome.

It was most likely the very tip of an ancient volcano.

As she lost the remaining altitude, she made minor adjustments to prepare for a landing within or nearby the island's protected waters and the beach. Through the windshield, she was granted her first glimpse of the island that might just pluck her from the possibility of death by ditching in the sea.

The volcanic dome curved to form a giant U at least half a mile in width. The beach was shaped like a large mouth, its white sands stretching open wide, like the smile of a Cheshire cat. It funneled into a large grotto beneath the rocky outcrop, the tips of the U-formation nearly touching. It left a sliver of land less than twenty feet wide through which a tidal river of turquoise water flowed into the inside of the larger body of a sheltered lagoon.

Amelia banked to the left, extended the flaps to full, and lowered the landing gear wheels.

The Electra glided across the edge of the beach. She pulled back on the wheel, lifting the nose until the aircraft flared. The Electra fought to maintain lift for a further second or so, before succumbing to gravity, and stalling.

Her wheels touched the thick sand, and the Electra rolled to a stop.

Amelia climbed out, grabbing her Kodak 620 Duo camera.

She took a photograph of the Electra with the backdrop of the strange volcanic island in the background. Somehow, whatever happened, she felt there needed to be a record. Even if she didn't survive, someone would one day find her, and she wanted that person to know the truth.

In the sand, white as snow, were a set of footprints that led east, toward the half-dome shaped remnants of the ancient volcano that now overhung part of the beach like the mouth of a behemoth monster turned grotto. But the shipwreck drew her attention. The wooden remains of a 16th century Dutch Fluyt, with its distinctive pear-shaped hull — most likely used in early exploration of the Southern Seas — rested half buried in the sand. She'd seen drawings of the same type of vessel in old maps produced by the Dutch East Indies Company. It must have washed up on the beach long ago.

Amelia took a photograph of the shipwreck.

As she walked around the back side of the half-buried hull, she spotted that the glass fitting that adorned the captain's aft cabin had long since shattered, allowing a clear line of sight inside. She made a cursory glance, knowing full well that the wreck was far too old to offer anything of any useful assistance to her.

The hollowed eyes of a skeleton's skull stared back at her.

Lying next to the wretched remains was a broken chest. The iron had rusted through, revealing a hoard of gold coins which had now leaked out, scattering along the cabin floor. It was a bounty fit for a king.

She put her hand to her mouth, and stepped back, knowing full well that it would serve her no better than the crew who had died on the island as castaways. Amelia expelled a deep breath of air, hoping that she wouldn't share the same fate as the Dutch explorers.

If the gold had remained untouched all these years, it meant one thing — she was the first visitor to the island since the demise of the Dutch ship.

Where the hell am I?

Not one to give up on anything, Amelia continued to follow the footsteps which led toward the cavernous opening in the volcanic structure.

She crunched her face up tight and swallowed down the fear that rose in her throat, as she noted that all of the footprints led from the shipwreck to the cave, with none returning to the beach. Her gaze traced the deep lines of the footprints to a section of rock where three separate stones, each as large as a bus, jolted together to form a natural archway. Her eyes landed at the entrance. There was something ominous about an opening that descended underground on a deserted island, where others had entered and likely never returned.

Amelia mentally closed her mind to the idea. After all, she was on a deserted island somewhere in the South Pacific. Nothing dangerous was lying in wait for her.

She stepped through the arched gateway.

A set of stairs had been carved into the brittle volcanic rock. It looked like a medieval stairwell, spiraling to the left with the precision that she doubted few stonemasons could recreate today. She set her jaw and with an equal mixture of awe and curiosity, Amelia descended deep into the subterranean tunnel.

Her descent continued for an intangible duration.

Light filtered through glassy rocks, allowing enough ambient glow to make out the shape of the tunnel and the location of the stairs, but little else. She placed her left hand on the smooth, glassy surface, using it for guidance and balance.

The effort that someone had made to construct the strange stairwell amazed her. Her ears hurt as she continued her descent and she found herself swallowing to equalize them.

How far below sea level can I be?

She would have given up and returned to the surface if there was anything to return to, but the fact was the medieval masonry staircase, like something out of a fairytale which led deep into the Earth, was her only hope.

Amelia stepped around the next bend and her left hand came free of the cold stone wall. She stopped, blinked more than once, as if doing so would remove the haze of disbelief.

The stairwell ended on a giant rocky ledge that overlooked an underground prehistoric world to rival anything Jules Verne had imagined.

The ceiling in this new vault was so high that it could only be seen at the edges of the wall and not in the middle. A warm ray of sun shone down from above on the entire subterranean habitat, making her feel like she'd just stepped out into the great expanse of an ancient savannah. Giant trees and plants were covered with fruits she had never seen before, filling her nostrils with the scent of rich fragrances.

Her eyes swept the near-mythical environment with wonder. It was impossible to tell where the place began and where it finished. It might have been a small country in its own right. Thick rainforests, including giant gum trees, more than a hundred feet tall, filled the area. There were massive open plains of grass, and a freshwater river that split the ancient world in two, with multiple smaller tributaries and streams that ran off from it.

An 80-foot waterfall raged somewhere to the east, sending a fine mist down upon the valley. The sound of birds chirping echoed throughout. Ancient megafauna, oversized mammals, drank by the bank of the river.

To her left, a beam of light filtered through the subterranean vault above, shining light the hue of purple, and lighting up the image like an exhibit at a museum — on seven faces of what looked like ancient cavemen. Her eyes locked on the mysterious faces. They were almost human, yet nothing quite so advanced.

She picked up her Kodak 620 Duo camera, aimed its lens on the remarkable image, and snapped the shot.

Her lips curled into an impish smile.

Where in God's name am I?

Within an hour of the Electra's last confirmed radio transmission, the *USCGC Itasca* launched what would soon become the world's largest and most expensive sea and air search operation in history. The *Itasca* undertook an ultimately unsuccessful search north and west of Howland Island based on initial assumptions about transmissions from the aircraft. The United States Navy soon joined the search and over a period of about three days sent available resources to the search area in the vicinity of Howland Island.

The initial search by the *Itasca* involved running up the 157/337 line of position to the north-northwest of Howland Island. The *Itasca* then searched the area to the immediate northeast of the island, wider than the area searched to the northwest. Based on bearings of several supposed Earhart radio transmissions, some of the search efforts were directed to a specific position on a line of 281 degrees from Howland Island without evidence of the flyers.

Four days after Earhart's last verified radio transmission, on July 6, 1937, the captain of the battleship *USS Colorado* received orders from the Commandant, Fourteenth Naval District to take over all naval and coast guard units to coordinate search efforts. Naval aircraft from the Colorado were directed to the Phoenix Islands seven days after Amelia Earhart and Fred Noonan went missing. One of the Phoenix Islands, an uninhabited atoll that ran directly through the 157/337 sun line, named Gardner Island, showed signs of recent habitation. Yet despite repeated circling and low flying, pilots were unable to elicit a response from anyone on the island.

Despite an unprecedented, extensive search by the U.S. Navy—including the use of search aircraft from an aircraft carrier—and the U.S. Coast Guard, no traces of Earhart or Noonan, or their Electra, were ever found.

Until now…

CHAPTER ONE

Mediterranean Sea, Present Day

T HE CABIN OF THE PHOENIX Airlines Flight 318 was uniquely silent. There was no talking, the entertainment consoles were switched off, and none of the flight crew were making their way through the aisles. The only noise that could be heard was the quiet drone of the A380's four Rolls-Royce Trent 900 engines as the aircraft cruised at 38,000 feet.

Andrew Goddard stretched uncomfortably awake in his economy-class seat. At six feet seven inches, his protracted frame was far from what the designers of the Airbus A380 had in mind when they planned the economy-class seating for optimal passenger numbers. At sixty-one years of age and with his wealth, he thought he was beyond this sort of physical mistreatment.

Through a large inheritance, and success as a rare antiquities dealer, Goddard had obtained the sort of grandiose wealth that couldn't be spent in a lifetime. Despite this, he could have passed as a monk. His long, wispy gray hair was tidily swept back and he wore a trim, almost white beard. He had an ascetic face, with bony features and a protracted jawline. His intelligent blue eyes were so pale they were nearly clear. Looking down his long nose, as he took in the aircraft cabin at a glance, trying to guess how much longer it would be before they landed.

Andrew blinked, trying to remove the haze so thoroughly embedded.

He had been sleeping fitfully over the last couple hours or so of the long-haul flight. Uncomfortable, and heavily sleep deprived, he'd taken a glass of cognac in the hope that it would give him the few hours rest he so desperately desired.

Instead, all it had done was fill his mind with vivid nightmares.

He hated to fly.

Fact was, if he'd been given more time, he would have caught a ship, as daft and old fashioned as that might seem. Not that it mattered. The point was moot. He'd found out less than fifteen hours ago about the auction.

It was the first time in his lifetime the item had come up. Almost certainly the last opportunity he might have to see the ancient relic.

No. He would gladly suffer the discomfort of modern flight to be there.

He checked his watch.

It read 10:30 a.m.

He'd left LaGuardia International in New York at 6:55 p.m. Andrew tried to make sense of the time differences. Italy was six hours ahead of New York. That meant they had been in the air for a total of nine hours and thirty-five minutes.

The flight was supposed to have taken just eight hours and fifteen minutes.

They should have landed at 9:05 a.m.

So what went wrong?

He was almost certain he'd calculated the time-zones wrong.

Do you turn your watch forward or backward, when traveling east? Venice was six hours ahead... or was that behind New York? Had his watch automatically updated, aligning itself with an incorrect time-zone?

He smiled, feeling the sudden staccato in his aging heart settle into something entirely more sustainable.

Andrew shook his head. It was nothing more than the combination of the cognac playing tricks with his head and his watch updating to the wrong time-zone. *That should serve him right buying into the new digital watches.*

He shifted. They would be on the ground soon.

Still, his back hurt.

Goddard distracted his mind with thoughts of Venice.

It was quite interesting this time of year. The celebration of Carnival of Venice had passed and the Catholic city would become hushed, almost dead silent. But soon Easter would occur and the metropolis would spring to life again, with crowds flocking to the churches to celebrate masses. Places with a strong religious tradition tended to have a more marked sense of the weightiness of the passage of time, as well as a calendar year broken up by at least one celebration a month, just to keep that weightiness from becoming too boring. But then the people had always needed their bread and circuses. A religion that didn't understand *that,* wasn't a religion or a culture, that endured.

He was arriving on Good Friday, which was a few days before the Easter celebrations began. And fortunately, even though he hadn't been able to obtain a decent airplane ticket, he did have a reservation at the Hotel Antico Doge in the Cannaregio district. The hotel had a gondola entrance and was appointed as though the proprietors expected a member of the House of De Medici to arrive and demand a room: gold leaf, velvet, silk patterned wallpaper, parquet floors, crystal chandeliers, all sorts of luxury. It had been built in the former palace of Duke Faliero, who was executed for attempting a coup d'état. The service was excellent; Goddard had stayed there twice previously, most memorably on a trip the previous year to assess the legitimacy of a "lost" piece of art by Titian.

The painting had proved a fake, but the trip had not been a complete loss. He'd met someone who had heard of a third *Eternity Mask* — an elaborately adorned ancient stone mask of unimaginable value. If the legends were to be believed, the Gods had forged the masks out of stone, spreading all seven of them — one for each continent — throughout the world, so that one day they might be joined together to reveal the path to true enlightenment.

Goddard wanted to stand up and stretch, but he was certain they would be arriving any moment. He checked his smart watch again, which had in fact automatically updated itself to local time. He recalled once again that the scheduled arrival time was at 9:05 in the morning, Venice time.

It was now ten forty-five a.m.

No, that couldn't be right. He slipped his leather briefcase onto his lap and pulled out his smartphone to check the time. The phone and watch must have slipped out of sync somehow.

Ten forty-five.

That still didn't seem right. His watch might have updated automatically, but his phone had been on flight mode, which prevented any updates from occurring.

He licked his lips, and then slid his briefcase back onto the floor. It struck something at his feet, which he bent over to pick up. His fingers brushed a heavy-bottomed glass. It was his empty cognac glass. It must have fallen while he was asleep. He grunted as he tried to twist his too tall body into an angle that would let him pick it up.

As he straightened up, he bumped into his neighbor's knee.

"My apologies," he said.

The man, who was both too tall *and* too wide for his seat, was asleep, head lolling against the seat back, mouth open and breathing heavily. Clearly, he hadn't been disturbed.

Goddard checked the time again.

They should have landed nearly two hours ago.

In fact, if they didn't land soon, he'd miss the auction.

He had moved heaven and earth to make it onto *this* flight. He couldn't miss the auction. *Could not.* It was the opportunity of more than a lifetime. The first opportunity in three lifetimes!

Therefore, it couldn't be ten forty-five.

If the plane had needed to be rerouted due to some issue, they would have announced it over the speakers, and he would have awoken. He was sure of it. A single cognac wasn't enough to knock him out *that* firmly.

Goddard sniffed the glass, but he had drunk the cognac hours ago. Now the faint scent coming from the glass was more or less drowned out by the necessary smells produced by eight hours of being packed like sardines into the economy section.

The man next to him was still out, and the miniscule old woman just past him was more or less invisible, hidden by the man's bulk, but she, too, appeared to be asleep. In fact, the entire cabin seemed to be under a hush. He looked out the window. Underneath him was clear sky and the wine-dark sea, or rather what he suspected was the bluish-purple of the deepest parts of the Adriatic.

Oh God, how I hate to fly!

He stretched awkwardly in his seat. The man next to him wore a titanium watch on his left wrist. With some luck, Goddard would be able to make out the position of the hands on the watch without waking the man. It was three-quarters-past the hour, all right, but he was having trouble seeing in what direction the hour hand was pointed.

Goddard leaned down — under the guise of tightening his shoe laces — so that he could get a better view of the watch.

Ten Forty-Seven...

"Good God!" Andrew said, his deep voice resonating jarringly throughout the cabin.

He turned, prepared to apologize for his outburst, but no one seemed interested.

The cabin creaked under a bit of light turbulence. It was a big, new aircraft, and he'd been hearing what sounded like a haunted house creaking and groaning around him the entire flight, which had prevented him from getting much sleep.

He couldn't have slept that deeply.

Part of him raged that he hadn't been awakened in order to hear about any changes in flight plans. Part of him questioned the situation. Something was fundamentally *off* about all this.

If nothing else, not only were all the people he could see asleep, but the entertainment screens on the backs of the seats were dark, and, in his experience, that never happened. The airlines like to keep ads running at all times.

He pressed the button on the bottom of the screen to call a flight attendant, and also to check the time.

The screen stayed dark.

His throat tightened.

He stood up. "Excuse me?"

The corpulent passenger next to him had slouched down in his chair so that his knees were pressed up against the seat back in front of him. He'd removed his seat belt as well. Goddard looked around. Everything seemed unnaturally quiet and still.

His pulse quickened. "Can someone please tell me what time it is in Venice?"

No response.

In fact, it wasn't just the seats surrounding him in which the passengers appeared to be asleep… but all the seats he could see. Every screen dark, every head slumped over in its seat.

What the hell is going on?

He clenched his jaw and pressed the call button again. His

screen remained unresponsive. Despite his cool, blank-faced exterior appearance, his heart was skipping more than the occasional beat.

Goddard had once had a dream that he'd been flying in an airplane and it had disappeared from around him, causing himself and the rest of the passengers—even the flight attendants and the pilots—to enter freefall. The flight attendants were still pushing their drink carts, and the passengers, tumbling end over end as the wind tossed them around, smiled and shouted things like, "Do you have that in diet?"

He had screamed himself awake.

I'm still dreaming, he realized.

He had fallen asleep after drinking that cognac and now he was having a nightmare in which he was late for the auction he so desperately needed to attend.

He suppressed a grin.

It was rare that he was aware of his own dreams at the time he was having them. Rudely, he climbed over the large man's legs, not worrying whether he jostled or woke the man—he would disappear as soon as Goddard woke up. He shoved past the old woman next to him, a much easier task.

He wandered the aisles of the plane, smiling and nodding at the sleeping passengers.

Goddard could do literally anything he wanted. None of this was real. He tweaked the nose of a man with a priest's collar, but other than that he resisted the temptation to interfere with any of the other passengers. Instead, he walked to first class and checked the cabinets. They were locked. He found a flight attendant dozing in her seat and took her keys out of her pocket, sorting through them until he found the one he wanted for the clearly-marked alcohol cabinet.

He poured himself a cognac and swirled it around in the bowl. Now this was the way to have a nightmare. Before he put the keys back in the flight attendant's pocket, he checked her watch. The watch, faithful to the dream, now stipulated that it was 10:45 a.m.

It didn't matter.

He walked to the front of the plane and jiggled the door. It was locked, which was somehow reassuring, but something niggled at him.

He looked back over his shoulder. Now he was looking into the first-class section.

What was it? What was dragging at the back of his mind?

His eyes narrowed.

He'd missed something perfectly obvious.

There was no one in the first-class seating area except himself, two flight attendants, and…well, no one. He snorted. His subconscious hadn't bothered to populate this section. Maybe because he wanted to take all the seats himself!

What a strange dream…

But wait.

Something else, an almost irrationally unimportant detail, stuck out at him.

The window covers were up. That wasn't right. The clocks worked well enough, but his subconscious had gotten that detail wrong. He concentrated. For the dream to be perfectly accurate, the side of the plane facing the sun should have had most of the window covers down.

Nothing moved.

Odd.

Weren't things like that supposed to fix themselves, in a dream? Poof, just like that? But then, he hadn't run into a single surreal element in the dream, not since he'd awakened and found himself here.

Was he in a dream?

He pinched himself. It hurt. But that wasn't conclusive. He hopped up and down on the floor, trying to convince himself to float a little. Nothing. He even winced and tried to make the plane disappear around him.

It didn't.

Am I dreaming or awake?

There was one test that should be conclusive. In all the dreams he'd ever experienced, he could never read. He might stare at a newspaper or a book in a dream, but even his dream self couldn't make real words appear. There was something un-dreamlike about the act of reading itself.

He leaned over and pulled a book out from behind one of the empty seats. It was a Stephen King novel named The Tommyknockers, which simultaneously confirmed the fact he was having a nightmare, while proving he was awake.

Goddard's eyes began to water, as if they didn't want him to trust the evidence of his own senses. He blinked them clear, then opened the book.

The letters were there in all their quintessential 1980s horror.

It wasn't a dream.

He wasn't dreaming.

Goddard dropped the book. His pulse quickened and his skin was covered in goosebumps.

It was after ten forty-five in the morning. Everyone in the plane was unconscious, including the flight attendants.

He swallowed, dropped the book, and walked over to the nearest flight attendant, the one whose keys he had taken. She was still unconscious. He shook her by the shoulder.

"Excuse me, ma'am." He squeezed her shoulder hard in an attempt to wake her. "Do you know what happened?"

Her head flopped limply on her shoulders as he shook her. He dug his thumbnail into the meat between her neck and shoulder, a move that should have brought almost anyone out of a deep sleep.

No response.

His eyes swept around the first-class area. At the end of the aisle, just before the curtain into the business class area, he spotted a first aid sign. He opened the overhead locker. Inside it was a first-aid kit. He let that drop to the floor. Behind it was a portable oxygen tank, a small C cylinder. Attached to it were a regulator and an oxygen mask for medical emergencies.

He pulled them out carefully, checked the connections, then twisted the top of the cylinder. Goddard listened to the faithful hiss of oxygen free-flowing. He placed the mask over his face, and took a couple of long, sweet breaths.

The entire cabin appeared to be unconscious, which meant there must have been some sort of environmental catastrophe on board the aircraft. His mind jumped through the most likely causes — a sudden depressurization, the release of some sort of toxic gas, or a mass poisoning of their water supply with sedatives and or even hallucinogens.

As he breathed the cold oxygen, Goddard felt the muddled thinking from earlier start melting away. His heart steadied. He was getting control of the situation. Now all he had to do was make sure that the pilots were all right. They should be. The cockpit was separated from the rest of the plane for a reason.

Besides, they had an emergency supply of air or oxygen… or something to specifically prevent this sort of thing happening to them, didn't they?

He glanced toward the door.

He walked on stiff, unyielding legs toward the locked cockpit, as he carried the small oxygen cylinder with him. It felt as though he would faint. The world at the edges of his vision had turned gray. He took a few breaths from his oxygen mask, but that made things worse.

You're hyperventilating.

Slow your breathing.

For a few moments he stood on the far side of the cockpit door, panting. The gray edges slowly receded.

He was fine. He was going to be fine. It was all going to be fine.

He tugged on the door again. It was still locked.

He banged on the door with the side of a clenched fist. "Excuse me? Open up, please. There's been an emergency back here, and I need to speak with someone."

No response.

He tried looking through the peephole, but it was useless. All he could see was the back of the pilot and copilot's chairs. Next to them, he could just make out a couple of bright smears of light, and another shadow.

He banged on the door again.

Nothing.

He glanced around the empty cabin, looking for something with which to open the door. Even as he searched, he knew the search would be futile. Cockpit doors had been made a thousand times more secure after 9–11. There was no reason for anyone to have left a handy crowbar or fire axe lying around nearby.

He had a moment of inspiration and retrieved the flight attendant's keys; however, none of them fit the door, either. Another perfectly sensible precaution.

But there had to be a way. Otherwise, how would anyone be able to help the pilots if, for example, someone managed to plant a canister of toxic gas in the cockpit?

If he could only calm himself, he would discover something. He was sure of it.

He walked back toward the center of the aircraft, looking from side to side over the heads of the sleeping passengers. The window covers were all up in this section, too.

Finally, he reached the main galley at the rear of the plane, where the flight attendants had prepared the economy-class "meals," which were little more than microwaved TV dinners, along with a self-sealed cold salad.

He searched the drawers nearby. The cutlery was plastic. He checked his watch. It was just after 11 a.m. now. He didn't have time for this! Any of this! A flash of rage swept over him. *It was probably already too late.* He started throwing the contents of the drawers on the floor. He knocked over the cart.

The airplane might crash.

But what did it matter. If he'd missed the auction he might as well be dead. He certainly wouldn't get another chance within his lifetime.

No, he needed to get control of the aircraft, and then use the radio to stop that auction. He ripped out another drawer. It contained nothing of any use to him. Unless he wanted to try breaking into the cockpit with a bottle opener, he had found nothing of use.

He swore.

If he wanted to hide something from the passengers, where would he put it? He frowned. He was missing something else significant…

He walked back to the front of the aircraft. He had circled around it several times but hadn't registered what it meant: a set of stairs leading upward to the second deck of the aircraft. He wasn't on just any aircraft, but an Airbus A380, a behemoth of a jet whose upper deck was dedicated almost exclusively to first-class and luxury-class seats.

He hesitated. What could he possibly expect to find on the upper deck? The access to the cockpit was on this level.

The pilots and crew needed to rest somewhere, didn't they? They couldn't be expected to work the full flight without a break.

He remembered hearing once…somewhere…something about a small, secret compartment close to the cockpit where pilots and crew could stretch out and take a nap.

The door was tucked behind the cupboards where the drinks were kept, and it was locked. *Cabin Crew Only*, said the official label, along with a laminated sign taped to the door that said, *This is not a passenger toilet!*

He tried the flight attendant's keys on the lock. One of them worked.

A steep set of steps, almost a ladder, led downward. Goddard descended them carefully. Two bunks were tucked to one side, along with an emergency phone to the cockpit. A small toilet, a storage cabinet, and a refrigerator completed the hideaway. He had to squeeze to fit inside the narrow spaces and duck constantly to keep from hitting his head.

Goddard picked up the phone and pressed the call button. The red light flashed, but nobody answered.

He looked for any way to get into the cockpit. No dice. Probably the pilots had a similar area of their own, underneath the cockpit.

One of the keys unlocked the storage cabinet.

Inside it was a fire axe.

Aha!

He pulled out the axe and climbed the narrow stairs. Trying to manage both the sharp axe and the handrails necessary to pull himself up the stairs was awkward, but he managed it.

At the top of the stairs, the door had swung closed again. He cursed. It wasn't locked, but the latch was somewhat stiff. He wedged the axe between his feet on the steps and gave the door a shove.

It swung open, banging on the cockpit door, then swung closed again.

Goddard froze for a moment. Outside the open door, he'd glimpsed something that had changed since he'd gone down to the crew area.

But what was that change?

It was only the sense of emergency that had let him notice the detail. If he'd had less adrenaline in his system, he might not have noticed anything.

A young man was now sitting at the window seat farthest away from the secret door to the aircrew rest area. Goddard raked the previously empty first-class cabin with his eyes, landing square on the new arrival.

There were no other new additions to the first-class passenger's cabin. He opened the door again, gently.

Goddard studied the man. He couldn't quite see all of him because of the position of the two seats in front of him. Instead, all he could make out was the tip of the man's clean gray sneakers, which rested on the extended footrest of his first-class seat. The sneakers stood out because they were some sort of name brand sports shoe that looked more like they belonged on an astronaut than a basketballer. They weren't just gray, they appeared almost metallic. The sort of thing some rich kid would wear to look cool.

Holding the axe, Goddard climbed the rest of the way out of the rest area to get a better look at the new arrival.

In jarring contrast with his sneakers, the man looked like a typical Ivy League graduate. Well groomed, blond hair, parted on the right side. Clean shaven. He wore a blue-gray Burberry slim fit business suit that reeked of old money. The top of his shirt had been loosened at the neck along with his dark hound's-tooth-patterned tie. His skin was well tanned, but Goddard imagined that came from a recent summer vacation as opposed to any outdoor vocation.

"Excuse me, are you awake?" Goddard asked, watching for any reaction.

The passenger didn't move at all.

Goddard persisted. "Sir… are you awake?"

The younger man's head lolled to the side, causing the stranger to snore.

Was the man putting it on for show, or was he really asleep? Goddard replayed the mental image of walking into the cabin from a few minutes ago. He was certain no one had been in the first-class cabin. In fact, Goddard recalled, he had taken specific note of it at the time because he'd been unable to book a first-class seat, and had discovered the entire cabin empty.

So, if the passenger hadn't been there a few minutes ago, how did he get there?

Carefully, Goddard walked up to the man and nudged his leg with one foot.

No response.

He shouted, "Hey! Are you awake?"

Not even the slightest flutter of an eyelash. Goddard gave the man a firm shake, then pinched the skin sharply with his thumbnail between the thumb and forefinger. The skin went white, then red. The man didn't wake.

If he was faking it, he was doing an *incredibly* good job.

Goddard growled, "I'm going to beat the shit out of you if you don't answer me, you bastard!" He raised the axe overhead, as if to strike the man.

Who continued snoring.

No, he was truly out cold.

Had he been carried here? Or… somehow… fallen down the stairs from above and ended up, perfectly arranged, in the downstairs seat? Or had Goddard simply missed the man the first time round? That was probably more likely.

Goddard looked up the stairs but saw no movement above. He could check, but…no. He was out of time.

He turned toward the cockpit door and raised the axe to attack it. But the blade never struck the door. It didn't have to.

Goddard suppressed a grin.

The door was slightly ajar.

What the hell's going on?

He carried the axe in his right hand as he grabbed the door handle in his left. The door opened easily.

Maybe the man with the sneakers was a pilot, despite his lack of uniform… and maybe he had just stepped out of the cockpit and become incapacitated by whatever was causing everyone else within the cabin to become unconscious.

"Excuse me," Goddard said, tentatively as he opened the door wide. "There's been some sort of emergency back here. We need help."

There was no reply.

He stepped inside.

The cockpit of the A380 Airbus had two main seats, each surrounded by a plethora of equipment, switches, dials, buttons, and warning lights. Each seat supported what looked like a computer terminal showing various readouts.

Nothing seemed out of the ordinary. No mysterious cloud of smoke or other gasses filled the air. No red lights flashed. No alarms went off in an attention-attracting fashion. In fact, both seat harnesses were still buckled.

He opened his mouth to speak to the pilots, but instead gasped.

Because the entire cockpit was empty.

CHAPTER TWO

GODDARD STARED AT THE COCKPIT.

Electric switches lit up everywhere the pilot and co-pilot could reach, from the walls to the ceiling. His only understanding of the cockpit of a modern aircraft — *any* modern aircraft — had been derived from the movies. He wasn't going to be able to intuitively work out how to land the thing. The sheer number of dials and switches made that unimaginable. An iPad sat on the copilot's chair, next to which was a pair of thick user manuals in the middle of the cockpit, looking like a couple of phone books — a firm reminder of how much information was likely to be inside.

The hair stood up on the back of Goddard's neck.

He was starting to really feel like he was stuck inside some sort of sick and twisted Stephen King novel. He made an involuntary shudder as fear rose in his throat like bile. Something inside him, a sixth sense, told Goddard to close the bomb-proof cockpit door and lock it immediately.

Goddard turned quickly, half expecting to see something evil already standing there. He had learned long ago not to argue with his instincts. He closed the cockpit door and slid the security bolt into the locked position.

Confident the cockpit was now secure, he stepped close to the door and peered out through the peephole, looking around the cabin. Nothing had changed. Mr. Sneakers was still asleep.

Goddard expelled a breath. He was now alone in one of the world's most advanced cockpits, with enough specialized equipment and electronic switches to fill thousands of pages worth of aircraft manuals — but at least the cockpit was secure.

The question was, now what could he do?

Goddard sank to the floor with his back to the cockpit door. It was starting to sink in that he was never going to reach the auction. That opportunity was gone. Fact was, it was highly unlikely he would ever get the aircraft safely on the ground.

It had come down to a matter of life and death now.

He took a few deep breaths to try to help clear his mind. He had to be realistic and focus on survival now. Opportunities in the art world, he reminded himself, came and went.

The responsibility to join the *Eternity Masks* would have to be passed on to someone else.

He'd heard somewhere that pilots spend less than ten percent of their time at the controls, physically flying the plane. Most of that wasn't even in the air — it was while the aircraft taxied to its runway, on the ground. Despite that, he wasn't going to delude himself that it would be easy to maneuver the behemoth modern aircraft. Using the proper settings, the aircraft itself could take off, land, and maintain a straight and level flight. But it still took pilots years, if not decades, to know when and how to set those computer systems.

The lines across his brow deepened as he frowned.

None of that was going to help him though, because he didn't have a clue what the proper settings were…or which switches and buttons to use to engage any of them.

But maybe there was someone out there who did.

He stood up. They'd been in the air for what…ten… eleven hours — if he'd calculated it right. He didn't have enough time to go through the manuals before they ran out of fuel. But hanging in front of the pilot's and co-pilot's seats were two headsets.

He'd never flown a plane, but he had used a two-way radio before. All he had to do was get hold of someone who could direct him how to bring the aircraft low enough to increase the oxygen level… if he could do that, surely someone else on board — any of the five hundred some passengers and crew — would know how to land the plane.

Goddard swallowed hard and tried to put the thought of how many lives were at stake out of his mind. Sitting down in the pilot's seat, he strapped himself into the awkward harness, and tightened it, reassuringly.

He put the headphones on. In the middle console between the two seats was the one panel in the sea of controls that he recognized: the radio.

He wasn't sure what the frequencies should be, but each channel had an "actual" and "standby" frequency already set up. He could only hope that the channels were set up to transmit and receive information locally.

He depressed the transmit button.

But found that nothing would come out of his throat, it was so tight. He released the button, coughed, then tried again.

A hoarse croak came out.

"Mayday, Mayday," Goddard said, recalling every movie he'd seen with an aircraft incident. "This is Phoenix Airlines flight number 318. We have an emergency and we need help."

Emergency didn't seem to cover the weirdness of the situation.

He released the button and waited.

After a moment, a voice answered in a heavily accented, sickeningly calm, English. "Phoenix Airlines flight, can you repeat your aircraft number?"

Goddard swallowed.

If he hadn't been strapped in place by his harness, he would have slumped over with relief. Someone had responded. Maybe even someone who knew what was going on. It wasn't much, but it was something. It meant he was no longer all on his own. The responsibility for nearly five hundred passengers and crew no longer rested squarely on his shoulders.

One thing was certain; the air traffic controller was going to have a much better idea how to handle the situation than he did. They must have procedures in place, people to call, resources to draw upon, maybe even a nearby military fighter jet that could be scrambled to help guide him through everything and stay by his side.

Goddard took another breath.

Actually, he didn't care *who* he was talking to. Not yet. He'd made contact. That was step one. Step two. He needed to find out how to take the plane off autopilot and reduce altitude.

"This is Phoenix Airlines flight number 318 from LaGuardia to Marco Polo, Venice. We have an emergency and need assistance."

There was no response this time.

His hand hovered over the switch that would have swapped the actual and standby channels. Maybe he should try the other one. Maybe he'd just moved out of range. But the voice had sounded crisp and clear.

He told himself to be patient. They had to be calculating and triangulating his location or something—*they can do that, right?*—trying at lightning speed to figure out the nearest landing locations.

After thirty seconds that felt more like thirty minutes, he couldn't stand it.

He tried again. "Hello? Are you still there? This is Phoenix flight 318. I'm the only person conscious on the plane...I don't know if the plane depressurized at some point or...what happened. Everyone else on the plane is out cold. I'm just a passenger. I have no idea how to fly this plane and I need help.

Can anyone hear me? I need someone who can explain this to me, step by step. I need to know exactly what to do. There are a lot of lives riding on this. Please help me!"

His throat was tightening again. He'd lost contact. He was going to die. He let go of the transmit button and waited.

It was all he could do.

After a few seconds, the same calm, strangely accented voice responded. "Sir, we treat this sort of hoax with the utmost severity. I don't know how you accessed this channel, but if you abuse it again, we will have you arrested and formally charged."

Goddard was set back.

What the hell?

In desperation, he tried to explain himself.

He tried to speak. Choked. His tongue was too dry to talk.

"Sir, this is Phoenix flight 318. I don't know what you're talking about…this is a serious, genuine emergency. This is not a prank. I need help, or this entire plane full of people is going to crash. There must be hundreds of people onboard." His voice sounded strained over the headset. "I'm not lying. I need help. I woke up out of a dead sleep and nothing is…nothing is right."

The voice responded in an angry tone, "Sir, we are calculating your radio position. You will be formally charged for this unauthorized intrusion into our channels."

Goddard shouted, "This is not a hoax! Why can't you understand what's going on? We're going to crash, and you're treating me like I'm some kind of lunatic!"

There was another pause.

Goddard felt his heart beating in the back of his ears as he inadvertently held his breath.

The voice replied, "Sir, Phoenix Flight 318 crashed three days ago!"

Goddard felt his chest constrict, his whole body slumped forward, for a moment he couldn't breathe. "No! That's impossible!"

"I don't know what you're trying to do," the air traffic controller said. "But they've already located the wreckage. There were no survivors…"

CHAPTER THREE

ACOLD GUST OF AIR blew across his heart, turning his blood to ice.

Sickened, Goddard went limp in his seat.

Crashed?

Dead?

What were they talking about?

He refused to accept it. He didn't necessarily know what he believed happened to you when you die, but one thing was certain, this was neither his Heaven nor his Hell.

It was as though someone were playing a joke on *him.* That had to be it. He'd reached a…a radio enthusiast, who had taken the opportunity to screw with the luckless bastard begging for help. It was monstrous. He switched to the standby channel and repeated his call for help.

No one answered.

After a few minutes, he switched back to the original frequency and tried again. This time, there was absolutely no response.

He was screwed.

He had to work out how to disengage the autopilot, lower it to 5,000 and then reset the autopilot.

There was no other choice.

He stared at the instruments around him. Most of them were identical on either side of the cockpit. Pilot's half, co-pilot's half. That meant he had half as many things to worry about. Radio panel, check.

Goddard glanced at the fuel gauges. They showed the aircraft nearly full. That must have been impossible. They had been flying for more than ten hours, yet they had barely used any fuel whatsoever.

No aircraft was that efficient.

It was all impossible — unless…

Had they landed and refueled somewhere while everyone was asleep?

He shook the thought from his head, filing it away for a future problem to solve — if they made it through the current disaster.

Goddard continued to scan the gauges and controls.

The compass pointed south. They were heading due south. Good. He glanced at the map. He was over water. Most likely the Adriatic Sea, but could they be somewhere else entirely? It didn't matter. His job wasn't to land the aircraft. No amount of automated assistance was going to make that possible for him. His job was to bring the aircraft down until the air stopped being so thin. Let someone else work out where they were and how to land the aircraft once they woke up.

He fixed his gaze dead ahead, imagining himself flying the aircraft. If he were a pilot, where would his attention be? The most important controls would be right in front of him and beside him, easily within reach, and capable of providing important information without hesitation or distraction.

One small screen directly in front of him fit that description.

It showed a circle, half brown, half blue. If he had to guess, and he did, he would say that was something like…a plane leveler? It looked like the Airbus was on an even keel, with no dipping or tilting. The small screen beside it looked…kind of like the radar screens that you saw in movies. Nothing went blip or ping on the screen. That was good, but it also reminded him that he was still all alone in the world.

Below the screen were the letters PFD. It was obviously some sort of display screen, giving vital information about the aircraft. Goddard felt if he had the time, he could work out what each of these things meant. He pulled up the iPad and typed in the name at the bottom of the screen—PRIMARY FLIGHT DISPLAY.

The iPad brought up the simplified instructions relating to that device.

He ran his eyes across the information sheet…

The center of the PFD contains an attitude indicator (AI), which gives the pilot information about the aircraft's pitch and roll characteristics, and the orientation of the aircraft with respect to the horizon.

He finished skimming the information quickly, devouring any information about how to keep the aircraft straight and level once he'd lowered it to 5,000 feet. It was good knowledge and useful information, but he found nothing that mentioned the autopilot—and none of it would be relevant if he couldn't take the aircraft off autopilot.

Goddard looked around for the autopilot settings. *Anything* marked autopilot.

Nothing.

His hands were shaking now. He forced himself to relax. Nothing was flashing. He wasn't yet out of fuel. Nothing was *wrong* with the plane, exactly. Trying to act before he had a clear idea of what was going on would just potentially cause the plane to crash.

He went over all the buttons and switches again. Nothing

marked autopilot.

He swallowed.

AP, he would look for something marked *AP*. A lot of the switches and buttons had abbreviations on them.

A couple of different buttons were marked *AP*. *AP1, AP2,* and something on an overhead panel marked *APU*. The overhead buttons didn't look like they were the vital functions of flying the aircraft, though. Things like "Entertainment," "Ext Lt," and "Anti-Ice" options. And "Eng Start," but the engines were already running, so he wasn't going to muck around with that one.

AP1 and *AP2* it was, then. *AP1* had a green light on the button. An autopilot program was engaged.

In order to land the plane, he'd have to turn that off. Not yet, though.

Within a few minutes he'd picked out the pedals on the floor, the joystick, and a kind of handle in the middle of the center console as looking important. Unlike movies that he'd seen, there wasn't a misshapen steering wheel in front of the pilot and co-pilot's seats, but a keyboard that folded up under the panels. He slid it carefully back into place.

The joystick must…change the plane's direction? Up and down, right and left. That seemed to make sense. Despite his age, he'd played computer games which used a joystick once or twice. He just wished one of those games had been a flight simulator. No matter, he could only work with what he had. The pedals must be for the gas and the brakes? Except that he had some kind of vague memory that the pedals didn't control the gas.

He was panting for breath. Shit…he'd put his oxygen tank down. He found it beside the seat and took a few breaths, but not too deeply. He didn't want to hyperventilate again, either.

The handle in the center console. That was the…gas. The throttle…whatever the term was. He was pretty sure of it. It was labeled 1,2,3,4 Engine Master.

He steeled his resolve, gripped the joystick—which felt entirely inadequate for the controls of the world's largest airplane—and flicked the AP switch to off.

Bracing for a sudden dive, he realized that nothing had happened. The aircraft continued to fly straight and level, while the engines hadn't changed their pitch whatsoever.

The autopilot was still running.

That didn't make sense. *What the hell did I just turn off if not the autopilot?* Goddard didn't wait to find out. Instead, he flicked the AP switch back to on.

Scanning the instruments and controls, he couldn't spot anything.

He was out of luck. His body slackened into the chair. Years ago, a friend had taken him sailing on a *Beneteau 42* in the windy waters of San Francisco. Despite the concept of men against the wild, they had used an autopilot to steer the yacht. Halfway through the day, a large cargo ship crossed their course, and his friend was forced to take control of the helm. Goddard thought back to that day. How did his friend do it?

Goddard grinned at the simplicity.

He didn't turn anything off. He simply took control of the wheel. The autopilot had a built-in safety feature that allowed human inputs to override the computer.

Could it really be that easy on board an A380?

There was only one way to find out.

Goddard gripped the joystick in his left hand and gently maneuvered it forward. The attitude indicator in front of him showed the position of the aircraft's nose dipping below the artificial horizon. The airspeed indicator started to increase, while the altitude decreased. The vertical speed indicator, next to the altitude indicator, displayed his rate of descent in "thousands of feet per minute." For example, a measurement of "+2" indicates an ascent of 2000 feet per minute, while a measurement of "-1.5" indicates a descent of 1500 feet per minute.

Right now, it was displaying a rate of negative 5 with a red light lit up next to it. Goddard had no idea what was considered an acceptable rate of descent, but apparently 5,000 feet per minute wasn't what the engineer's at Airbus had in mind for its A380.

Goddard applied gentle backward pressure to the joystick and the rate of descent reduced to 2,000 feet per minute. The glow from the red light disappeared.

He adjusted his position on the joystick until it balanced comfortably around the 2,000 mark, and let the aircraft continue its descent until it reached 5,000 feet. At that point he gently maneuvered the joystick until the nose was resting level with the artificial horizon.

Goddard then let go of the joystick.

The aircraft continued flying straight and level. The autopilot, having accepted no further human inputs were being given, continued to maintain control.

He grinned.

They weren't kidding when they said anyone can fly these things.

He waited and watched the PFD and other gauges for a few minutes to make certain the aircraft wasn't going to simply fall out of the sky without his input. The compass kept them pointed due south. No reason to change that, he guessed. When he was confident the plane was indeed flying itself, he unclipped his harness, stretched and then opened the cockpit door.

He froze.

Because, the first class was empty. The man with the suit, tie and running shoes had disappeared. Andrew hooked the door latch to the side of the cockpit passage, so that the door remained opened. No longer restricted by carrying the oxygen cylinder and keeping the mask on his face, he ran through the aisles toward the tail end of the aircraft.

"Hello!" he shouted. "Is anyone awake?"

No response.

"Please! We need help. There's been an accident. Can anyone hear me?"

His voice echoed down the empty cabin, but there were no replies.

Goddard made his way aft, toward business class.

Row upon row of luxurious seats were empty. Not a single person—passenger or crew—was there.

No! No! Where did everyone go?

He glanced out the window. They were still above the clouds. He started running toward the tail.

"Where have you all gone!" he screamed.

But only silence and the hum of the jet engines returned to him. Economy class was empty. Andrew reached the tail end of the aircraft.

Losing control for the first time, he shouted,

"Come back you motherfuckers!"

His world was really spinning now. *How could they have all gotten off the aircraft during flight?* What the hell was he missing?

He ran the sweaty palms of his hands through his hair and slowly walked back to the cockpit. So what if they'd all left him? They were unconscious before. It wasn't like any one of them was going to help him. They may as well have been dead. They were no use to him.

He grinned. It was sardonic.

If he was going to make it out of this whole thing alive, he would have to put the damned aircraft on the ground himself.

He was a smart guy. The aircraft used computers. He didn't know a thing about jets or flying, but he knew computers. With confidence bordering on insanity, he thought, *I can do this!*

Andrew reached the end of first class and stopped at the door to the cockpit. Fear rose in his throat like bile, and the tingling sense of Death teased at his spine.

Because the cockpit door he'd made certain to lock open so that he didn't accidentally lock himself out, was now closed.

No way! It can't be!

He pulled on the handle. It didn't move. He then peered through the security hole.

There was a man at the controls. The plane was no longer on autopilot. Someone was actively steering the aircraft.

He banged on the door.

"Let me in!"

The man made no reply.

"I have to know… please, just let me know what the hell is going on?"

While keeping one hand on the joystick, the guy turned his head, looking straight at him. It was the man with the metallic sneakers from before—the one he was certain had moved, who was wearing a suit with tie and running shoes. He was right, the man had moved before—not that it was going to help him any. It was now impossible to get inside the cockpit. The aircraft's only axe was lying on the floor inside the locked cockpit.

Goddard yelled, "Just tell me know what's going on…"

The stranger turned and looked at him. The man's dark eyes were wide like a pair of saucers, they focused on him. The man smiled, put his finger to his lips as if to quiet him, and whispered, "Shush."

As though all that yelling might wake the other passengers. A moment later, silent as always, the man turned to face the windshield. He carefully adjusted the controls and actively steered the aircraft on a brand new course.

Andrew screamed…

"I just want to know what's going on!"

CHAPTER FOUR

Queen Maggie Mine, Colorado

J ESSE MCKENZIE SWITCHED ON THE old diesel generator.

The engine sounded like someone shaking a bucket full of loose nuts and bolts until it warmed up, before finally settling into a resonant drone that comfortingly filled the shaft. The ventilation fans started to turn. Nearly a minute went by as he waited until water started to flow from the twin extraction pipes which ran out from the descending tunnel. Content that the water pumps were working, he picked up his hard hat, switched on the helmet light above his forehead, stepped in through the rickety adit, and commenced his descent into the underground mine shaft.

At sixty years of age a lifetime spent down the mines had changed him from what his natural genetic disposition had determined. Despite being nearly six foot tall, he appeared short and stocky. Unlike the giant "show muscles" of a professional bodybuilder, he had stocky, undefined muscles that worked like the hydraulic mining machines nearby, exerting extraordinary strength compared to their size. He had a hard face with a strong jawline, that matched the rest of his body. His deep-set eyes, the same color brown as what remained of his still thick brown hair, appeared hooded like he had something to hide. Deep lines creased his furrowed brow, revealing the despondency of a man who knew his way of life was already over, but just refused to accept it.

He had the kind of mining experience that, in previous generations, would have made him a valuable foreman. But that was back in the days when experience meant something and long before mining had turned to automation for everything and anything, leaving jobs few and far between for an old man nearing retirement.

It was nearly three years to the day since the largest of the mine's gold veins had abruptly ended as fast as it had begun, and the company went bust. Six hundred miners had walked out that day and no one but him had been back ever since. He had worked nearly forty years at the Queen Maggie Mine. He couldn't imagine working anywhere else. All the equipment had just been left there to rot. There was still gold in the mountain. It doesn't just disappear overnight. The problem was it becomes less profitable to mine. Commodity prices fluctuate. Automation had changed everything, making some winners and many losers. Sometimes it's no longer viable to run such a big operation. He figured a smaller group would buy it soon enough.

Until that day, he might as well keep mining on his own terms. He thought he had a pretty good nose for sniffing out gold. It would be trespassing and then stealing if he was lucky enough to find any gold worth taking—but he figured it was okay. They still owed him two week's pay. It may as well be severance.

The Smith and Rochford mining company had hung onto the property as part of its portfolio, hoping that more efficient mining and processing techniques would be developed to make extracting the last traces of gold profitable.

As it was, gold mining was an expensive operation. It was almost impossible to make money digging the rock out of the ground by hand. *Almost* impossible. But all the easy veins had been found and extracted a century or more ago. Then all the easy veins of other metals — silver, lead, copper, coal, molybdenum, aluminum, zinc, even a little iron — had been tracked down.

Improvements in technology had led to strip-mining, that ugly process of peeling off layer by layer of rock and running it through processors that chemically broke down the minerals, atom by atom, and left them at the bottom of a pool of toxic sludge.

Nobody could deny the method was *efficient*.

But it still wasn't efficient enough to make the Queen Maggie Mine profitable. Not if the machines chewed up the mountain and spat out every atom of gold.

The original owner, John D. Blair, had gone bankrupt trying to extract every last bit of gold in the mine in 1910. Smith and Rochford had bought up the mine and had managed to eke out a profit until three years ago.

Since then, the rock had sat idle.

The gold ore that was still in the mountain wasn't even a matter of faith, but of record.

Jesse reached the end of the tunnel where he'd been working the night before. He ran the beam of his helmet light over an intricate web of quartz. Most of it was entirely useless. There was gold in there, for certain, but at such low quantities to make it entirely worthless to extract. It was a delicate operation. He was following the quartz reef trying to sniff out the most viable vein to work. Without heavy machinery, he had to be very specific with his targeted mining. He stopped and, using a pickaxe he'd left leaning against the wall yesterday, he chipped out some of the grayish quartz from along the end of the shaft.

Then he inspected it with his helmet light.

The stone was light gray with paler flecks running throughout. It was an ugly stone, the kind that always reminded him of half-melted and refrozen snow mixed with dirt. "Snirt," they called it as kids, and "snirt rock." But as a miner, he had learned that this was the stuff of magic.

He flipped the piece of quartz over.

Several flecks of gold greeted him. In an entire ton of it there might be half an ounce of gold—if the mine was an exceptional one. More often, one might have to go through twenty tons of gold ore in order to pull out an ounce of the stuff, which would be worth about $1300 dollars, or just over $21,000 per pound. The gold bars that one saw in movies about stealing gold from Fort Knox were 400 troy ounces of gold—or about 25 pounds each. One gold bar, half a million dollars…and at least 800 tons of ore stripped out of the ground. The calculations making gold worthwhile to take out of the ground were delicate and situational.

He kissed the "snirt rock" and shoved it in his pocket. He'd keep it as a lucky piece.

Then he picked up the pick and swung again. He had no intention of digging an entire ton of gold ore out of the mountain by hand, but it felt good to get into the rhythm of the swing. Chips of rock flew all around him. Under the pick, the song that the rock was singing changed slightly. He frowned, then took off his goggles to examine the rock more closely.

If he didn't know better, he would have said the black rock in front of him was obsidian.

It was as strange as finding, well, a volcanic silicate in the middle of a bunch of quartz crystals. Colorado had several known sources of the stuff, but they were all much farther to the north or south of the state. No, wait. There was some down in a couple of mines near Nathrop, Colorado, only about fifty miles to the south. Wouldn't that be something, if the vein ran all the way from the Queen Maggie down there?

The vein of gold-filled quartz seemed to get richer as it mixed with the obsidian. He stepped back and studied the rockface. The beam of his helmet light reflected off the thick pieces of gold-encrusted quartz zigzagging through the black, glossy, volcanic stone that shone like a royal mirror.

It was a geological phenomenon he'd never even heard of.

This one find could be enough to make the past three years worthwhile. The seam of gold running into the obsidian wall appeared to increase in size and quality. He felt the pace of his heart quicken. Would it lead to the motherlode?

He was going to have to drill, bring down some explosives, and blast the obsidian out of his way. It would make some noise and someone might hear it, but it was unlikely anyone would come to investigate a strange sound coming from an otherwise abandoned mine.

Over the course of the next few hours he drilled several blast holes into the obsidian and filled them with ANFO, a mix of ammonium nitrate and fuel oil. He'd even put in a couple of sound-and-vibration dampeners, three-foot-thick layers of sand fill and another of aggregate. He was so far away from the blast that he didn't expect to hear it so much as feel it, through the rock underfoot. Even on the surface, however, he wore his safety equipment.

It was time.

He pressed the detonator and waited.

It seemed to take an inordinate amount of time. He strained his ears to catch the first hints of the sound. The light breeze and faint birdcalls seemed to roar in his ears.

Then he began to hear the deep, grinding sound of the stone breaking away underneath him. It seemed to reach him from every direction at once, not just at the opening of the mine shaft.

DANGER: OPEN MINE SHAFT KEEP OUT! EXTREME DANGER!

He smiled. The unimaginably *deep* sound coming out of the

mine shaft was music to his ears. It was a shame that all that obsidian was going to waste, but then it was going to waste anyway.

He waited until the rumbling had died down. Now came the waiting for the dust and gasses to settle. If a professional mining operation had been running this blast, it would have been easier and faster, with powerful air filtration units, motorized hauling and digging equipment, and other tricks of the trade. But for a solo operation, it was just him and a bunch of higgledy-piggledy equipment. He fully intended to clear the waste rock using a small ore trailer towed by a secondhand quadbike.

He stopped to have lunch, while he waited for the makeshift sprinkler system he'd rigged to do its job of grounding the fine dust that filled the mine shaft.

An hour later, and with the impatience of a much younger man, he switched on his helmet light and reentered the mineshaft.

The sprinklers had brought the dangerous fine particles down to an acceptable level. He switched the system off and stepped through.

He wended his way through the tunnel. The sides didn't look bad, not bad at all, although of course there was always a risk when blasting underground. The digger waited for him in front of a pile of aggregate. A hole at the top of the tunnel had revealed a clear area on the other side that had sparkled in the darkness, decorated with the glitter of shattered glass.

When he'd first looked through, he'd been exhausted. Too easy to make a mistake.

He'd backed out. Today was the day that he'd climb through.

He edged up to the hole, pushing a powerful flashlight, and a heavy sample bag. He said a little prayer and crawled through.

On the other side was a glass wonderland.

He cupped the top of his flannelette shirt over his mouth to filter some of the microscopic flakes of glass and quartz that still sparkled in the air. He got to his feet and began crossing the tunnel floor. It was intact, which was good news. The explosive had directed itself properly. He peered toward the end of the tunnel. He should have seen a face of gray quartz among the glittering black glass.

He didn't.

How deep did that vein run? Maybe he should have just switched to another mine tunnel. Well, as long as he was here, he might as well see what the fates had brought him.

The fractured obsidian glittered back at him.

Suddenly he stopped. Something was wrong about the tunnel.

He could hear himself breathing. In the confined space, every sound echoed back to him.

And yet...

He aimed the flashlight downward. The rubble at the bottom of the tunnel seemed to disappear for a few steps, then reappear again. He shuffled forward slowly, keeping a steady eye on the gap in the floor.

When he was standing next to it, he aimed his flashlight downward.

The unexciting, dull gray of gold ore lay just underfoot. Inconvenient, but it still put a grin on his face. Even through his goggles he could pick out a yellowish shimmer. There was gold down there in that rock, a fair amount of it, too, if he could see it from all the way up there—nearly twenty feet above. He must have blasted into a volcanic cavern that had formed millions of years ago.

It was too deep for him to climb down unassisted.

He gritted his teeth, and returned to the surface to collect a thick rope. It took him nearly an hour to get there and back, but it needed to be done. One false step and he would disappear down the crevasse, and, unable to climb out, he would never be seen again, his death remaining a mystery for years to come.

Jesse tied the thick fibrous rope off to a disused ore cart. The thing was made of iron, weighed more than a ton, and was permanently stopped at the end of the narrow-gauged line. He unfurled the rope, dragging it through the narrow opening of the new area the blast had revealed.

He threw the tail end into the narrow opening and carefully tested the rope, taking the slack out by tensioning it with his hands. It was nearly three inches thick, making it possible for him to climb it vertically if he had to.

Jesse fixed the beam of his helmet light into the opening and climbed down — real Indiana Jones style.

His heavy boots crunched the glassy rubble underfoot. He ran his eyes across the new obsidian vault. Holy hell. He'd dug all the way through the Queen Maggie Mine and now was encroaching on someone else's property.

And that couldn't be a good thing.

The beam of his flashlight struck the new opening, reflecting hundreds of small flakes, grains and nuggets of gold, which stood out on the black canvas of obsidian, like glittering stars in the night's sky.

He started to laugh.

It was big and boisterous.

There was enough gold there to make him rich. His life was about to be changed forever. Luck, like everything in life, turned on a dime. He was ready to kill himself, and now he was going to be rich beyond his dreams.

Jesse quickly started to grab the bigger of the nuggets, furtively securing them into his sampling bag, like a thief in the night. His heart pounded in his throat. He felt delirious with glee as he removed the piles of gold from the dragon's lair.

A moment later he turned the beam of his flashlight to the right and stopped laughing — because, there, embedded in the glassy obsidian wall stood a mask of what appeared to be an ancient caveman, with its hollowed out jade eyes glaring at him and its teeth grinning at him like some sort of heinous creature of the dead.

The stone eyes fixed on him like an ancient guard of some unimaginable cache of wealth, penetrating his soul, accusing him and cursing him for being a thief.

CHAPTER FIVE

J ESSE SWALLOWED DOWN THE FEAR that rose from his gut like bile.

With the sound of his heart pounding in his own ears, his breathing heavy, he wanted nothing more than to climb up the rope and run for his life. But what would that achieve? He would simply be throwing away all his riches. Despite the disturbing image of the mask, it was nothing more than that— an ancient relic of a superstitious people, most likely long extinct.

He forced himself to slow his breathing as he swept the rest of the obsidian vault with the beam of his powerful helmet light. The room was roughly ten feet long by fifteen wide and about thirty deep. It was secure. There was no other way in except for the opening in the ceiling through which he'd climbed down with the rope.

And no other way out…

Jesse tried to shut the thought out of his mind, fixing his mind on the immediate priorities. He could run away and return with… what? Some friends? He didn't have many and none whom he could trust with such a secret. Even those who would initially mean to be trusted would inevitably start spending their gold, throwing it around the town like they were rich… they would get drunk and then inevitably reveal that they had found a motherlode down the old Queen Maggie Mine.

Then what?

At best they would be forced to repay every ounce of it back to the rightful owners, Smith and Rochford.

If they pressed charges, they could end up doing serious prison time for stealing.

His wife, Betty might be a better choice. She at least knew how to be tightlipped. Still, if he were to sell his gold on the pretense that he'd made a secret discovery on a riverbed — somewhere he was going to refuse to give away in case other treasure hunters returned — it would be all the more believable if she didn't know the truth. If two people know a secret that meant double the chance of being found out.

No. So then what? Do I run scared, like a child afraid of the monsters hiding in the dark — or in this case, stuck within a wall of clear obsidian — or do I man up, retrieve the larger pieces of gold, and keep to the original plan?

Jesse swallowed and started to quickly fill his backpack.

It didn't take long. No more than ten minutes. He didn't bother with the small flakes. Just stuck to the gold nuggets, of which there were plenty. In a matter of minutes, he'd picked up more gold than he'd found in forty years of mining.

He strapped the bag onto his back. It was so heavy he had to lean forward to stop it from pulling him over.

Jesse took one more glance around the pile of fractured obsidian, quartz, and gold, shook his head in disbelief and started to climb the rope, hand over hand. He made it just four feet off the ground and stopped.

The strange mask was now at his eyelevel.

There was something accusing about the evil creature's

sinister glare. Yet something pleading too. Had it changed? No, that's impossible. The damned thing was frozen in obsidian for God's sake! Yet, where it had looked hideous and powerful before, like an unearthly guard over the riches of past kings, it now looked sullen and pitiful.

Jesse met its eye directly. "What?"

He half expected the creature to answer him.

When it didn't, he started to climb again.

At the top of the rope he climbed through the opening and dropped his backpack on the floor to catch his breath. The weight of the backpack made it harder than he expected. He was about to stand up and go, but something stopped him.

The mask was still down there.

Who made it? How old was it? Where had it come from? How the hell did it end up trapped inside a wall made of solid obsidian?

He gritted his teeth and, despite his fear, he climbed back down the rope to take a photo of the strange mask.

Jesse had no idea what it all meant, but was certain that one picture of it in the right places on the internet, would capture the interest of someone who might know.

CHAPTER SIX

Moab, Utah

SAM REILLY DROPPED ALIANA WOLFGANG off at the airport. He'd just bought a black 1989 Lamborghini LM002 in Los Angeles and was in the process of taking it to the east coast. He considered putting it on the back of a truck and having it shipped to his warehouse in Florida, which was attached to his private shipyard where his salvage vessel, the *Maria Helena* was ordinarily housed. But with the *Maria Helena* sunk and her replacement still being fitted out in the US Navy's Shipyards at Quonset, Rhode Island, he figured it was time for a road trip.

Despite being considered an antique, the Lamborghini LM002 was a solid workhorse. Kind of a cross between Sherman Tank and Formula One racecar. The four-door pickup, with a tubular steel frame and riveted aluminum body panels, was the Italian supercar company's first major departure from its better known, high-performance, hand-built, supercars.

He and Aliana had spent the weekend taking it through its paces in the four-wheel drive renowned Moab National Park.

She was originally going to come with him through to Colorado Springs to do some diving with Tom Bower and Genevieve Callaghan, but as things were, she'd been called back to the office to work.

Sam turned right onto I-70 and headed east.

He planted his foot on the accelerator and his entire body was thrown back into the seat as the V12 engine roared — the very same one used on Lamborghini's *Countach*.

Sam took genuine pleasure out of simply driving the antique vehicle, the same way an art collector might enjoy examining the brushstrokes of a bygone master. Of all of Lamborghini's forays into the increasingly popular SUV market, this was the only one he truly enjoyed.

It was the Italian car maker's third attempt at producing a military style vehicle, and the first to make it to an, albeit, short lived production. The Lamborghini *Cheetah* and the LM001, paved the way for LM002. But with both earlier models using rear-mounted American power plants and intended for military use, they were not well received due to their poor maneuverability. It wasn't until 1986 when Lamborghini decided to use a forward mounted *Countach* V12 engine that the vehicle took off for commercial production. Only recently, Lamborghini had made a fourth contender in the highly popular SUV market, with the *Urus*.

There was nothing wrong with the *Urus*, but of all of them, the LM002 was the only one that he could even imagine taking off road. It was rugged, sturdy, and built to drive like a tank — albeit a very fast one.

Next to him, his cell phone started to ring.

The LM002 was a couple decades short of having Bluetooth connectivity and handsfree. He squinted and looked up ahead. There were no cops, and no one else on the road.

He pressed the answer button and said, "Hello."

It was Elise, a good friend and one of his employees, a

renowned computer hacker. "How's your trip going? How's the new car?"

"It's been good," Sam replied, a slight grin forming on his lips. She was often so fixated on any task that she was doing that it was rare for her to start with a preamble. "The truck's good."

"That's nice. You needed a vacation. Where are you headed now?"

"Colorado Springs. I'm exploring some caves with Tom and Genevieve."

"Don't you do that enough for work?"

Sam shrugged. "It's what I do to relax."

Elise didn't get sucked into it. Instead, she said, "You're not going there now."

"I'm not?"

"No."

"All right." Sam asked, "Where am I going?"

There was an impish and excited tone to her voice. "The Monarch Mountains."

"Right."

"In Colorado."

Sam nodded. "Right. What am I doing there?"

"There's a miner out there who just posted a picture of a stone mask frozen in obsidian. The mask is identical to one of the pictographs of that make up the *Seven Faces*."

Six months ago, Sam and his team found an 8th continent. It had sunken into the Pacific Ocean centuries ago, but its highest points were on an atoll that nearly broke the surface of the ocean. The mouth of the atoll formed a natural grotto which protected an ancient beach. Inside, Sam found a perfectly intact Lockheed Model 10 Electra—the same type of aircraft that disappeared with Amelia Earhart and Fred Noonan on board during her attempted round the world flight. In the cockpit they found no sign of the renowned aviator or her navigator, but a

Kodak Duo camera. Sam had the film developed, and it revealed an image of a strange purple cave with a pictograph of *Seven Faces* of ancient humans.

"The same face exactly?" Sam crunched his face up, the muscles all going tight. "You've got to be kidding me. How can you be sure?"

"Facial recognition technology uses…"

"Okay, okay," Sam stopped her before she got into the technical aspects. If she was certain, that was good enough for him. "Where did he say he found the mask?"

"He won't say the exact location, but told me that he found it in an obsidian vault after blasting through a vein of quartz above. He said it was the only thing inside that hinted that the place had ever been seen by human eyes."

"How did he suggest the mask found its way in there?"

"He said he doesn't have a clue. That's what he's really interested in. Right now he thinks it's an impossibility."

"Where's the mask, now?"

"Still in the mineshaft."

"What?" Sam lips turned into a wry smile. "He just left it there?"

"He wasn't sure if it was an ancient Mayan Tomb or something… said he felt as though the mask was watching him. Said it scared the shit out of him to be honest. Like the fiend was guarding something, or about to curse him for eternity."

"All right, all right. I'm interested. Text me the address."

"Okay, will do."

"And Elise…"

"Yeah?"

"Can you please give him a call back and make sure he doesn't show it to anyone else or try to sell it before I get there."

"Will do, Sam."

Sam pulled over, put the location into the GPS on his phone, and pressed go.

He then planted his foot again, edging as far past the speed limit as he thought he could get away with.

It was a good drive.

And the car handled surprisingly well given its age and the fact that it had a curb weight in the vicinity of three tons.

At Grand Junction he took the exit turning onto Highway 50. It was a little before three p.m. when Sam drove into Sapinero, crossed the Gunnison River, and continued on west. The river ran through a mountainous valley. The highway meandered along the side of the river, sometimes changing its elevation by hundreds or more feet as the mountain range rose high above.

The road dropped as it came around a bend that led across a small bridge. Sam changed down the heavy gears and then put his foot on the gas as the Lamborghini started its climb up the steep slope of the mountain.

In his rearview mirror he spotted a number of motorcycles. They all looked the same. Yamaha YZ250 motorcycles, with their distinctive blue and white motocross coloring. The bikes were road legal, but far better suited to off road. Sam and Tom had ridden similar bikes on trails in their early twenties.

The riders, stuck behind him, seemed to quickly become impatient. Each of them took it in turns to try and overtake him, crossing narrowly between him and the oncoming cars. The highway meandered along the natural contours and undulations of the mountain range.

Sam braked heavily so that one of the riders, stuck in the deadly zone on the wrong side of the road while overtaking, was able to pull in front of him.

He came around the next bend and pulled onto the curb.

There were still three motorcycle riders behind him. They slowed down with him. Sam shook his head, wound down the window, and waved at them to pass. He eyed the riders, their faces invisible behind tinted helmets. They didn't move.

What the heck's wrong with you?

Sam pushed the gear into first, released the clutch, and floored the engine. The Lamborghini took off hard, accelerating up the next climb. The dirt bikes were fast, but with their nobly tires were not designed for the blacktop. The LM002 was much faster. Yet the riders fought to keep up with him.

Were they playing a game?

He squinted trying to split his time between watching what was ahead of him and the riders behind him. Up ahead, two more motorcyclists — the ones who had nearly been killed trying to overtake him earlier — seemed to have slowed right down, below the speed limit, as though waiting for him. As soon as he got close, they took off again, setting the pace to match his.

Sam put up with the game as the highway weaved in and out through a series of escarpments and valleys. The road narrowed, with a steep drop on the right-hand side, leading to the Blue Mesa Reservoir far below. The riders seemed to encroach farther and farther into his personal driving space — removing any doubt he might have that they were intentionally closing in on him.

The question was, why?

The riders seemed to surround him, blocking part of his vision ahead as well as behind. He swung the wheel to the right and the rider next to him backed off. In front of him, the riders stayed barely a car length ahead of him. Somehow slowing down, constantly forcing him to brake to avoid hitting them.

He was in a three-ton truck. What did they think was going to happen?

Sam glanced at his rearview mirror.

One of the riders was so close that the bike's front wheel seemed to disappear beneath the Lamborghini's utility tray.

He tapped the brakes, just enough for his brake-lights to glow red.

The riders dropped back for a moment and then opened their

throttles all the way to close whatever gap Sam had created.

The bikes moved with the synchronous precision of professional high divers. Coming in close and then parting.

Sam had had enough; he braked hard coming to a full stop.

One of the riders swerved and flew past him. Another one slowed to a stop right next to him, lifted his visor to meet Sam's eye.

Sam wound down the window. "What the hell's wrong with you?"

The man reached for a handgun strapped to the side of the bike's fuel tank.

Sam spotted it out the corner of his eye. He dropped the clutch and gunned the pedal, thankful for the Lamborghini's unbelievable acceleration off the mark.

The rider fired a couple shots, but Sam had already gotten ahead of the man, and the shots raked the back of the LM002's utility tray.

Now that any pretense of normal road rage was out, the riders seemed to race harder to catch him. Sam took the heavy truck from side to side across the lanes of the highway, making sure not to let any rider get close enough to the side of him to get a decent shot off.

A couple tried to shoot from behind, but they were wasting their time and bullets. It would have taken a near miracle to hit him through all the reinforced steel and tubular aluminum that made up the frame and paneling of the Lamborghini, Sam reassured himself, thankful that the Italian car company had originally built the truck with specifications designed to be pitched to the military.

Sam let his speed creep up, trying to outrun the slower dirt bikes. He was starting to get ahead too, when he came around the next bend, and found a large truck — an eighteen-wheeler — coming his way.

It had drifted onto his side of the road.

Sam jammed on his brakes, but it was too late. There was nothing he could do. He was going too fast. The heavy Lamborghini didn't have ABS and its wheels locked up, causing it to slide. He swung the wheel round the opposite direction, trying to control the slide, but it didn't work.

Instead the LM002 ran off the road, rolling down the near vertical embankment for nearly three hundred feet, bounding up and over a series of boulders, before being stopped suddenly by a large tree.

On impact, Sam swung forward, hitting his head hard on the truck's A-pillar, knocking him out cold.

CHAPTER SEVEN

J ESSE MCKENZIE WAITED PATIENTLY FOR his guests to arrive.

He had listed the image of the mask on a renowned archeology forum and had received interest from three separate parties, all of whom were willing to pay $10,000 just to examine the mask and inspect the site where it was found.

Rick Rodier, an archaeologist, Sandi Larson, an anthropologist, and Sam Reilly, a millionaire and a legend in the world of oceanography and marine recovery. The archaeologist worked with the University of Chicago, the anthropologist with Oxford University, and Sam Reilly — the youngest of the three of them, belonged to the Global Shipping Reillys. Each had their own reasons for wanting to examine the mask, but it was Reilly whose story most intrigued him, arguing that it was a worldwide concern.

In his email, Sam Reilly had said that he was also an amateur diver and had found something similar himself lately, and would pay handsomely for the opportunity to study the mask, and anything else similar that Jesse had found.

At 3:30 p.m. Rodier and Larson were the first to arrive at his house in Nathrop. They had met at the airport and hired a compact rental car together.

Jesse greeted them out in front with his wife. "I'm Jesse and this is Betty, my wife."

"Pleased to meet you," Rodier replied with a firm handshake. "I'm Rick Rodier. Professor of archeology at the University of Chicago. And this is Sandi Larson, from Oxford."

"Welcome to Nathrop," Jesse said, shaking Sandi's hand. "Nice flight?"

"Fine," Sandi answered, her eyes wide with genuine pleasure. "Wouldn't have mattered if it wasn't. For a find like this I would have crossed the Atlantic in a single engine biplane if I had to."

Jesse smiled brightly, revealing crooked teeth.

He was confident he'd found the right people to be examining the strange mask. He took the two academics in at a glance. The two couldn't be more polar opposites, despite both being at the top of their respective fields. Rick Rodier was tall, with the sort of comically lanky figure that almost looked like it had recently been released after spending too much time on some sort of medieval torture rack. His hair was salt and pepper, leaning more toward the salt than the pepper. He wore a kind smile and a friendly disposition on his face, which looked like it had been carved out of hardship, betraying every one of his eighty-two years of life.

In contrast, Sandi Larson was short with wide brown eyes, the same color as her hair. Despite her overnight flight from the UK, she looked bright, and vivacious. At just forty years of age, she'd already achieved tenure at Oxford in the faculty of anthropology. She had an athletic figure that suggested many of her years of study had been spent in the field. She was striking, a combination of intelligence, youth, and beauty that came close to paralleling his own wife some twenty years earlier.

Betty asked, "Can we offer you a drink or anything?"

"No thank you," Rodier and Larson replied.

Larson added, "I'm afraid we're both too impatient to see the mask to eat or drink anything. Do you know when Mr. Reilly is meant to get here? I had expected to see him at the airport."

Jesse shook his head. "Shouldn't be long now. He was driving on I-70 coming through Grand Junction when we spoke this morning. Said he was planning on driving through on his way to Colorado Springs tonight. Truth be told, I would have expected him to be here by now. Do you know him?"

"No, but I've read about some of the discoveries he's made in marine archeology over the years. He's got quite a reputation."

Rodier's brow furrowed. "Not all of it good."

Sandi made a slight grin. "Oh yeah, have you met him?"

"No. But I've heard things."

"Like what?"

"He's the son of shipping mogul, James Reilly. Like his father, he's a bit of a playboy. Spends a lot of time in exotic locations with expensive toy cars and beautiful women."

Jesse shrugged, thinking about his new-found wealth. "Hey, that doesn't sound like too bad a life if you have the money."

Rodier gave a small wave of his hand. "Real people in the world have to earn their way in life. It can't all be given. No one who ever significantly contributed to society had everything given to them."

Sandi folded her arms across her chest. "All right. Let's judge Sam Reilly by the sort of man we meet, not the one we've heard about. I for one am willing to give him the benefit of the doubt— at least until he arrives. You never know, maybe he'll be the first rich guy who's decidedly down to Earth."

In the distance, the sound of a powerful engine being gunned echoed throughout the mountain ranges.

Jesse glanced over his shoulder, and spotted a red Porsche Carrera 911 convertible, driving at least double the speed limit down the narrow residential street.

Sandi looked up and asked, "What is that?"

Rodier met her eye, grinning all the way. "That Ms. Larson, I believe is Sam Reilly — the first down to Earth rich guy you've ever met…"

CHAPTER EIGHT

S ANDI LARSON DISLIKED EVERYTHING ABOUT Sam Reilly.

He was handsome, for sure, but no amount of attractive physical features could make her warm to the man. Reilly was, as Rodier had forewarned her, everything that was bad about children brought up with unlimited wealth, starting with the fact that he raced down the residential street in a three hundred-thousand-dollar red sports car without any thought for the other road users he might just kill.

She ran her eyes across him.

His clothes were thoroughbred Ivy League — monogramed polo shirt, beige cargo pants, and a pair of hideous gray metallic sneakers that looked like they belonged to a popstar from the eighties. He was roughly six feet tall, with well-groomed blond hair, blue eyes, and cheesy smile full of evenly spaced teeth. His features were all classically patrician, as though good breeding and money could produce something worthy of Michelangelo's chisels. He was overtly handsome, like something out of the set of a Calvin Klein photoshoot.

Sam Reilly ran his eyes across her, too — making no attempt

to hide any lascivious thoughts he might have. He shook her hand, holding it for a moment longer than he should have, and said, "I see this ancient mask is not the only beautiful thing I get to see today."

She ignored the comment, turned to Jesse and said, "Okay. Now that we're all here, let's go see this thing."

Seeing her discomfort, Jesse nodded and motioned toward his old Dodge Pickup. "Come on, you can ride up front with me. The mine site is about thirty minutes from here."

"Sounds good."

She climbed into the front passenger seat, while Reilly and Rodier sat in the back. Jesse started the big diesel engine, and headed out along the same road they had come in on. About ten miles out, he turned off the blacktop and onto an old logger's trail. It took them up a steep embankment, leveling out on a narrow trail.

Sandi glanced at Jesse who, despite the thousand-plus foot drop over the edge, seemed undeterred. He had probably driven this route hundreds of times over the years. The thought reassured her. She wasn't afraid of heights, but she would have hated to die before getting the chance to see the extraordinary mask.

Her mind turned to the image of the mask she'd seen.

It was decidedly *Neanderthal*. Not Mayan, as Rodier had first theorized. Either way, it was about to disprove what was long held to be fact—that *Homo sapiens* were the first to cross the Bering Strait land bridge and colonize North America. Even if she was wrong and Rodier was right, it dispelled the long-standing belief that the Mayan empire only extended into South America and never this far into North America.

Whatever the case may be, it was going to be interesting to find out.

Jesse pulled up the Dodge next to the entrance of an old, seemingly abandoned mine shaft, set the handbrake and killed the engine. A derelict mine cart followed a dilapidated set of narrow-gauge railway tracks that led through an adit that looked like it had well since passed its use-by date.

Her lips formed a half-smile. "You found the mask in there?"

Jesse shrugged. "Afraid so, ma'am. Is that going to be a problem?"

Sandi opened the door and got out. "No problem. Just amazed that you're still working the old mine. Let's go."

"Very good."

Jesse handed out miner hard hats with attached flashlights to all three of them. He then reached down and started up his generator. Lights led in an irregular, lurching path down the tunnel, and a buzzing sound echoed up from the tunnel.

"Fans and pumps," Jesse told them. "Safety precautions. I have a multi-gas detector with me that'll start making an unholy racket if we wander into a bad patch. If that happens, I want you to turn around and climb out of the tunnel as fast as you can without endangering yourself. Just get the hell out."

There was a general murmur of agreement among all three of them that they wouldn't have to be told twice.

Jesse glanced at their faces, holding his gaze for a moment longer, and said, "All right. Then follow me."

Sandi took the hard-hat, switched on the overhead flashlight and followed him into the mine. Behind her, Reilly and Rodier were discussing the structural integrity of the old shaft. She didn't care. Jesse had told her he'd been down the mine for nearly forty years and had never had a problem. That was good enough for her.

She moved with a determined stride as she walked into the mine shaft, which ran straight into the side of the rock, gradually angling lower as it penetrated deeper into the mountain.

Rodier said, "Are you the Sam Reilly that discovered the Magdalena in Sweden a couple of years ago?"

"Yes," Reilly said. Jesse had no idea what they were referring to.

"Oh!" Larson said. "The airship! I've read a little about that!" And she started rattling off the story. In 1939, an airship took off from Nazi Germany with a number of wealthy Jewish passengers eager to escape the land of Hitler and the Kristallnacht. The airship had vanished for decades. A few years previously, Sam Reilly had discovered the airship…underground. The passengers had all expired, but the contribution that it had given to history was, as Larson said, incalculable.

Reilly let her ramble on. For some reason, as Larson spoke, he seemed to be getting more and more irritated.

They finally reached the part of the tunnel where Jesse had blasted, and the conversation stopped.

In an appalled voice, Larson said, "Oh, no."

"What?" Jesse asked.

"The roof has caved in, hasn't it?"

Jesse laughed and explained to her about using sand and amalgam to help muffle the blast, then showed her the passage where they would crawl through. "After I saw how much glass was inside there, I decided not to open it up any farther."

Larson crawled through, amazed by the glittering obsidian that covered every nook and cranny, even outside the wall of amalgam. That's how it was. Once you knew that a certain type of rock was there, it popped out at you everywhere. The trick, especially with gold mining, was to know what to look for in the first place.

Jesse stopped at a fork in the tunnel, pointing his flashlight to the right. "That's where we're headed."

Sandi glanced to the left where the main tunnel seemed to continue on. "Where does that lead?"

"About four hundred feet down."

She arched a dark eyebrow. "Really?"

"Yeah. Of course, it's mostly flooded now, but it was fully

operational up until three years ago when Smith and Rochford determined it was no longer a profitable run. I could get the pumps going again, and keep working down there, but truth be told, it would probably cost me more in diesel to keep the water out than I would ever find in gold. I can give you a tour of the gold mine if you're interested, or I could show you the mask..."

She nodded. "All right. Let's see where you found that mask..."

Jesse fixed the beam of his flashlight on a large opening of fractured obsidian. "It's through there, but mind your step. The blast took out part of the ground, leaving a wide hole that extends more than thirty feet deep."

"Okay, thanks. I'll keep an eye out for it."

"Make sure that you do..."

She ducked as she climbed through the opening. A thick piece of rope ran from a disused mine cart, through the gap and down the hole in the obsidian floor.

Sandi's eyes narrowed as they darted between the void and Jesse. "We've got to go down there?"

Jesse grinned. "Sure do… It's like the *Temple of Doom* all over again, hey?"

"It's too bad you had to blast," Rodier said. "I wonder if there had been any other artifacts."

"There wasn't any sign of anything on the walls," Jesse said emphatically. "I had no idea whatsoever, until I came down here after the blast. All I knew was that there was a plug of obsidian in my way."

"Did you find any gold?" Sandi asked.

Jesse crunched his face up tight, opened his mouth to speak and then closed it again.

"What is it?" she asked.

He made a little shrug, like she'd caught him out on a would-be lie. "I found some pretty worthless low-grade gold ore. The kind that isn't rich enough for the mining companies to bother about. That's why this place is abandoned."

"Ahh," she said, avoiding his gaze. There was no doubt the man was lying about something. She toyed with the idea of questioning him further, but decided against it. After all, what did she care if the man was stealing ore from a disused mineshaft? She said, "Let's see the mask! I'm dying to see whether it's *Neanderthal* or *Mayan!*"

He handed her the rope. "After you."

Her lips formed an incredulous smile. "We're just going to climb down the rope?"

"Sure, why not?" Jesse replied. "It's a thick rope; I'm sure someone like you would have no trouble climbing it."

"I'm not afraid of that… it's just…"

Sam Reilly said, "You can wait here if you want while we go look at the mask."

That was enough encouragement for her. "No, thank you. I think I'll go first, shall I?"

Jesse spread his hand out, motioning toward the rope. "Be my guest."

She climbed down, hand over hand. Reilly and Rodier followed immediately afterward, with Jesse climbing down last.

Sandi cast her eyes around the empty obsidian vault. It was magical on its own. Most likely forming after a large air bubble developed in the rich lava of an ancient volcano.

Next to her, Jesse shined his flashlight on the mask.

It was embedded — or more accurately, frozen — within a solid wall of clear obsidian.

She felt her breathing speed up. It was as though a feeling had come over them all, one that seemed to touch upon the mysteries of the universe.

The Great Pyramid of Egypt.

Stonehenge.

Easter Island.

And a mine shaft outside the Monarch Mountains, Colorado.

Behind her, Sam Reilly said, "Good God! It's true. You found one of the *Eternity Masks*!"

She turned to face him. "The what masks?"

"Never you mind." Sam already had a handgun out and level with her chest. "I want you all over there, where I can see you!"

"What the hell is the meaning of this?" Jesse said. "You won't get away with stealing the damned mask! What do you think, I'm an idiot? Betty knows where I am. If we don't come back she'll come looking with the sheriff."

Reilly said, "You can keep the mask."

Sandi backed up against the obsidian wall. "If you don't want the mask, then what did you come here for?"

"I needed to make sure it stayed buried forever."

Sandi asked, "What does an oceanographer care about an ancient mask staying buried?"

Rodier said, "I knew it. You're not really Sam Reilly, are you?"

The stranger with the gun shrugged. "Afraid not."

Jesse said, "Then who are you?"

"Someone who's devoted his life to keeping those masks buried."

Rodier spread the palms of his hands outward. "Okay. If that's what you want, we won't examine the mask. We'll just climb out and forget it ever existed."

The man kept his gun levelled at the three of them. "I'm afraid it's not that simple. I *really* am. I'm not a murderer. I didn't choose to come here and kill you. I did this for you, for everyone, really. If it makes you feel better, you can stay here for eternity to study the damned mask."

Rodier dived forward, jumping at the gun.

The stranger squeezed the trigger three times. Rodier cried out as all three bullets slammed into him, two in his chest, one just below his diaphragm.

Sandi dropped to the obsidian floor, holding pressure on the lower of the three gunshot wounds. There wasn't a lot of blood coming out of the top two wounds, but the third one must have severed a major artery — probably the abdominal aorta — there was likely nothing they could do to save Rodier. Even so, she held her hand on the wound as best she could.

In the scuffle, Jesse made an attempt to reach the handgun, but the stranger hit him in the jaw with his elbow. It was a solid blow. Not hard enough to knock him unconscious, but plenty hard enough to daze him.

Sandi looked up, but already the stranger was climbing the rope.

"Wait!" she shouted. "I need to know why…"

The stranger glanced down from the top of the rope and met her eye. "I'm sorry. Truly, I am. I wish to God Jesse had never found the mask. All I'm doing is what needs to be done."

"No wait!" she screamed.

But the stranger had cut the rope and disappeared, leaving them trapped inside the obsidian vault.

Jesse cursed.

Sandi noticed the blood had stopped spurting. She released her hand. There was no longer any need to apply direct pressure.

Rick Rodier was already dead.

There was nothing they could do for him. Not that it mattered any more, there was nothing they could do to save themselves.

Jesse squeezed her hand. "You tried your best. It's not your fault."

She closed her eyes and nodded. "I know."

"I wasn't lying when I said that Betty would come looking for us with the sheriff as soon as we don't return tonight. It might take a while, but they'll reach us. All we have to do is wait."

They did wait.

Not wanting to use up all their batteries before Betty came for them, they switched off their flashlights.

Time passed slowly.

Maybe an hour went by, maybe more. It was hard to say. But somewhere along the line, they heard a muted rumble. Their entire world started to shake in a giant earthquake.

Sandi switched on her flashlight. "What the hell was that?"

"He's blown the entrance to the mine!"

She felt that familiar sensation of terror rise again. "Oh, dear God!"

Without power the ventilation fans in the mine shaft above stopped turning. The drone of their whir ceased with deadly silence.

Sandi swallowed. "How long can we survive without the ventilation fans running?"

Jesse closed his eyes, gave it some thought, and said, "Two days. Three days at most. But I wouldn't worry about it."

"Are you kidding me, why shouldn't I worry about it?"

Jesse folded his arms across his chest and sighed heavily. "Because without power to the water pumps, these chambers are going to flood and we'll drown in about twelve hours."

CHAPTER NINE

S AM REILLY WAS *HURT*.
It felt like a giant had picked him up and shaken him until his teeth were loose. It wasn't a sensation he hadn't felt before. But it usually only happened when he woke up in the hospital.

He wasn't in the hospital.

He was in the driver's seat of his Lamborghini LM002. The large bull bar had taken the brunt of the impact as he collided with a tree. He peered through the windshield. A dirt trail ran just above the river only a dozen or so feet farther down the steep embankment. If he could get the truck started, he just might be able to maneuver his way down there.

That was, if he could get it started.

He turned the ignition. The V12 complained for a moment and then roared into life.

Sam grinned. Antique or not. The LM002 was built to last.

He shoved the gearstick into reverse. The low range reverse turned all four wheels. They spun for a spell, digging in deeper before gaining perch in the harder rock below.

The truck jolted backward.

It wasn't far. Maybe a few feet. Maybe a little less. It didn't matter. It was enough. Sam turned the wheel to the left, shifted the gear to first, and the LM002 lazily crept down the steep terrain in low-range gear.

Sam switched over to high range, put it in first, and drove forward. Ten minutes later he'd reached the end of the dirt trail, and was back on Hwy 50 heading east.

He picked up his cell phone and hit redial.

A woman answered the phone. "Hello?"

"Mrs. McKenzie?"

"Yes. Who is this?"

"Ma'am, my name's Sam Reilly. I was meant to meet your husband today to have a look at a mask he found buried in a mineshaft. I'm afraid I'm going to be a bit late…"

"I'm sorry, what did you say your name was?"

"Sam Reilly."

"I'm sorry Mr. Reilly; there must be some sort of mix up."

"Why do you say that?"

"Well, a Mr. Sam Reilly showed up hours ago and said he wanted to have a look at where the mask was found."

Sam planted his foot hard on the accelerator. "Where's that man now?"

"He's with my husband and some other archaeologists. Why, what's wrong?"

"How far's the mine from your house?"

She answered without hesitation. "Half an hour, why?"

"Do you have a gun?"

"Yes, of course we do. A Remington pump-action shotgun," she said, before adding as way of an explanation, "We live all the way out here on our own. Have to protect ourselves. Why? What's going on?"

Sam said, "I'll be at your house in twenty minutes. Bring your shotgun. We'll head up to the mine together."

CHAPTER TEN

J ESSE GRABBED THE DIAMOND BLADED drill he'd used to set the blast holes. He had brought it down into the obsidian vault earlier under the assumption that the parties interested in the mask were going to want him to fracture the obsidian wall, so that they could retrieve it. He just hoped that if he broke through the wall of obsidian it would lead to an opening. After all, someone must have gotten the mask down there in the first place.

He started the drill and quickly worked at the wall. He was up to his third drill hole when water started to flow down from above, cascading like a waterfall.

Sandi shouted, "What's taking so long?"

Jesse spread his hands. "Obsidian normally splinters. I don't know why it's not doing that here. I'm going to have to try some more drill holes."

"All right, all right. Just keep going! That water's going to rise fast!"

Jesse held the drill hard against the obsidian wall and kept its diamond bladed drill head turning. Next to him, Sandi attacked the wall with the pickaxe. Despite her petite size, she threw a considerable amount of energy and focus into the wall.

The water soon reached his knees.

When it was at his waist height, large fissures began forming down the length of the wall.

Sandi grinned. "It's cracking!"

"So it is!"

As the water reached their shoulders, the obsidian wall gave way to the mounting pressure. A large crack ripped through the wall, causing the volcanic stone to splinter in a spidery web of white, before shattering.

Sandi, unwilling to come this far only to lose the ancient mask, grabbed it as it came free and the wall shattered completely. Water rushed through to the second obsidian cavern on the opposite side, dragging them both along with it.

Jesse fought to stand up.

The water spread out over a larger area and was now no higher than his knees. He ran the beam of his flashlight across the walls of his new environment.

And then cursed loudly. "It's the same. We're still trapped."

Sandi held up the mask. "What a stupid way to die, hey? For some stupid mask…"

Jesse turned his gaze at the mask.

It seemed happier now that it was free. Like the genie let out of the bottle, it had regained some sort of sinister power. The damned thing looked positively evil as it sat their grinning at them in their time of torment.

The second cavern was larger than the first, but that didn't matter much. The fact was, there was still nowhere for them to go.

Unable to escape, Jesse focused on the mask again.

His eyes widened as he realized what he was looking at. "Holy shit!"

Sandi's eyes narrowed. "What is it?"

"The entire thing is made out of Alexandrite!"

"I'm sorry. I'm an anthropologist, not a geologist. What's Alexandrite?"

"Alexandrite is one of the rarest of all colored gemstones. It's a strongly pleochroic gem—meaning that it absorbs light differently depending on the position of the light. This creates the optical phenomenon of appearing with unique colors, depending on lights and angles. In particular, it exhibits emerald green, red and orange-yellow colors and tends to change from one color in artificial light to another in daylight. The color change from red to green is due to its strong absorption of light in the yellow and blue portions of the spectrum. Typically, alexandrite has an emerald-green color in daylight but exhibits a raspberry-red color in incandescent light. Fine faceted alexandrite over 1 carat is more valuable than sapphire, ruby or emerald."

"That's fascinating... So we're both going to die over a colorful, expensive rock that someone carved in the shape of an ancient caveman?"

"I don't know what to say..."

The water rose and as it did, they began to float, rising higher in the obsidian vault the higher the water rose.

Sandi floated on her back. "We're not going to drown; we're going to float to the top!"

"You're right!"

Ten minutes later, the water reached the opening through which they had originally climbed down.

Jesse climbed onto the floor above, fighting against the onslaught of the fast-flowing water, and then offered his hand to Sandi.

She gripped it in an instant, and he pulled her out.

He ducked down under the blast site and together they made their way to the main shaft. He turned left, and followed the tunnel another twenty feet up and stopped.

There, in front of him, the roof had collapsed.

It could take a week for someone to dig them out. It would take less than an hour for the flooding water to rise high enough to lethally greet them. All they had done was delay their deaths. It was a case of too little, too late.

They were both as good as dead.

Jesse waited in silence for Death to come for him.

To his surprise, Sandi stayed fixated on the mask, as though somehow by breaking its hidden purpose she might get to escape from her mortal prison.

But the water continued to rise.

It was soon up to their necks once more. Jesse swam to the side, where a small upward shaft had been dug out. It didn't go anywhere, but it allowed them another few minutes of precious air to breathe.

Flooded, their helmet lights began to flicker.

Jesse's failed first, followed by Sandi's a minute later.

Left alone in the cold and dark they both prepared themselves for Death.

Jesse McKenzie wasn't a very religious man. Instead, he grounded himself with a set of moral codes. He tried to do what was right and had succeeded in doing whatever he thought was right by Betty, but right now, he just wished he'd listened to her when she told him that the mask would do nothing but cause their family harm.

"I'm sorry, Sandi. This is all my fault."

"No, you couldn't have known someone would kill to protect this damned mask. It's not your fault. I'm just worried that the stranger was telling the truth."

In the dark, Jesse's lips managed to form a slight grin. "What difference does it make, now?"

"All the difference," she replied. "That man looked genuinely sorry he had to kill us, but said the world needed the mask to be buried. Now, after we drown, your wife will come here and when she does, someone will discover the cave-in. A day, a week, who knows how long after that, but somewhere, they'll get through. Then, when they find the mask—then what happens?"

Jesse laughed. "My goodness, Sandi. You are one of a kind! We're about to drown, and still, you're more worried about the rest of the world."

Sandi gave a strangled laugh of her own. "I suppose you're right. It's crazy. But after all, our value is in how we leave the world behind—better or worse. Our lives are finite compared to the human race. I have to believe that we have a purpose, more important than ourselves."

"That," Jesse said, "I can believe in."

He closed his eyes again, wishing the water didn't rise so fast, so that he could spend longer talking to this extraordinary woman. As it was, the water rose at speed. Already their heads were less than a foot off the ceiling.

He opened his eyes and imagined a bright light coming up from the murky depths below.

Jesse tried to blink the haze out of his befuddled mind.

He was certain he was becoming delirious when Sandi said, "What's that light doing?"

"What light?"

"The one below us. Down there! Can't you see it?"

Jesse blinked again. The dim light was still there. Only it was brighter now. It was growing. Racing to meet them.

Maybe this was how the whole Death thing worked…

Suddenly, a hand reached out from the light, followed by a mask.

A SCUBA diver surfaced.

Sandi's eyes widened. "Sam Reilly!"

The man nodded, "At your service."

Jesse asked, "Where the hell did you come from?"

"The Queen Charlotte Mine… I'll tell you all about it, but if it's all the same to the two of you, I'd like to start moving you both to the next cavern, before we all drown. Who's first?"

Without hesitation, Jesse said, "You go first Sandi, I'll wait here."

Sam nodded. "Don't go anywhere. I'll be back as soon as I can."

Jesse nodded. He was thankful that the man could save Sandi's life, but knew it was too late for him. The water was rising so fast it would be over his head within minutes.

He watched the light disappear.

The shaft between the Queen Maggie and the Charlotte mine had been flooded years ago. It must be more than a hundred feet long. Far too long to swim, and even longer with a second person sharing the same regulator and dive tank.

No. It was kind of Sam to give him hope, but both men knew all along that it wasn't possible. He was going to drown here.

All alone.

But Sandi Larson would get to live — to make the world a better place.

And for that, he could die happy.

Alone and in the dark, he waited to die.

But Death wasn't interested in him, yet.

The water continued to rise. He tilted his head back, treading water, and pushed his mouth toward the ceiling to take the last few breaths of his life.

On the fourth breath, he took in a small drop of water.

It made him cough violently, he needed air, but the fact was the mine shaft was all out. Only water remained.

Deprived of oxygen, his mind panicked. I don't want to die. Not like this! Not like this!

He opened his mouth to scream…

But instead, someone shoved a regulator's mouthpiece between his lips.

He took a deep breath. He never imagined air could taste so divine. Like Lazarus before him, his mind embraced the euphoria of those raised from the dead.

CHAPTER ELEVEN

S AM SURFACED OUT OF THE water into the dark confines of the Queen Charlotte Mine.

It was a horizontal tunnel that had once joined the Queen Maggie Mine until its gold rich reefs ran dry, making it unprofitable to run. Betty, Jesse's wife, had explained to Sam that her husband had let it flood, after realizing that the reef was barren and that it would cost him more than he had to maintain the series of pumps to keep it dry. He'd tried for a while, but soon gave up, having realized the process was impossible.

Next to him, Sam had to coax Jesse to stand in the shallow water. Without a dive mask, all the poor man had been able to do was keep his eyes shut and entrust Sam to keep passing him the mouthpiece for the regulator as they had made their way through the dark confines of the flooded tunnel.

Upon realizing that his feet were touching the ground, Jesse stood up, wiped his face, and made a silent prayer of thanks.

Sam stepped out of the water and shined his flashlight down the horizontal tunnel. Leaning with her back against the edge of the wall was a woman shivering in the cold. It was the first time he took any notice of her, having originally concentrated all his effort onto swimming through the flooded tunnel to save Jesse.

Now, he took notice of her.

She was shorter than average, with long red hair, blue eyes, and a steely gaze of defiance. She had dried herself with the towel he'd left with the rest of his dive equipment and wrapped a blanket around herself. Her white-skin was covered in goosebumps as she shivered slightly, but despite her apparent cold, she appeared unharmed by her near-death experience.

"I'm Sam Reilly," he said, "I'm sorry, I didn't quite have the time to catch your name earlier."

She stood up and offered her hand. "I'm Sandi Larson."

Sam cocked an eyebrow in recognition. "Professor Larson, the anthropologist from Oxford University?"

"Yes, that's me." She smiled. "But please, call me Sandi."

"I read your dissertation on the evidence of *Homo erectus* within North America 130,000 years ago after the analysis of the *Cerutti Mastodon Site*, near San Diego in 2017. It was fascinating…"

"Thank you." She sighed. "It wasn't my project. I was there to offer my clinical analysis of their uranium-thorium dating process. Even so, I was proud to be part of the team. That was why I was so keen to see this site first hand. I believed this might have been the crucial evidence we needed to confirm our theory about the original migration of *Homo erectus* into the Americas, long before *Homo sapiens* reached the continent."

Sam nodded. "It will be interesting to find the truth. I have my own theories about how that mask arrived here, but we'll discuss those once we get out of here and you've had a chance to study the artifact."

She frowned. "The mask was lost in the obsidian chamber."

"I'll need more air," Sam said. "But we can always go back and retrieve the mask."

"That won't be necessary," Jesse said, ruefully, as he revealed the mask from a small carry pouch.

"You dragged that all the way through the submerged tunnel system?" Sam asked, incredulous.

"Sure did. I figure anything someone just tried to kill me to hide, needs to be exposed so the whole damned world can see! That's my way of dealing with people like that."

Sam picked up the rest of his dive gear, packed it in his backpack, and slid it onto his back as he slid his arms through the shoulder straps. "Sounds good. Let's start heading back to the surface before we freeze to death. We're still another hour from the surface."

"Great idea. I'd feel happier once we're above ground," Sandi said.

"We both do," Jesse said, standing up.

"You're welcome. It was just good luck I got here in time more than anything."

Jesse's face contorted with confusion, like he just remembered something peculiar. "How did you find us?"

Sam finished drying his face. "I called your home phone to tell you that I'd been in a car accident. When your wife answered, she informed me that another Mr. Reilly had already gone off with her husband and two archeologists. She was the one to pick it up first, and asked if there could have been two Reillys."

"That's Betty for you. Impossible to pull the wool over her eyes about anything."

"So, she took me up to the entrance to the Queen Maggie Mine, where we immediately discovered the cave in. When I asked her if there was another way in, she replied that there wasn't, unless I wanted to swim through about two hundred feet of flooded mine shafts. That's when I decided to make the dive while she went to the sheriff for help."

Jesse squinted his eyes. "But where on earth did you find scuba gear in the mountains?"

Sam shrugged. "It's my gear. I was actually on my way to Colorado Springs to go diving, searching for some old aircraft wrecks in the lakes there, when I heard about your discovery. It was just good luck I had all my equipment in the car when I arrived."

Sandi raised her eyebrow. "Another historical expedition?"

"Not really. Just a good friend and I catching up on a much-needed vacation."

"You search for lost aircraft in icy lakes to relax?"

Sam nodded, sheepishly. "It's what I do."

They continued walking in silence for several minutes until they reached a fork in the tunnel. Sam shined his flashlight down in both directions, before glancing at his compass to confirm the route that led to the surface.

He turned to the right, following the standard US narrow-gauge 3-foot 6-inch minecart track as it snaked up the tunnel toward the surface. As he flashed his light to the left, he noticed with rising confidence that there was no railway track, which suggested the tunnel terminated nearby.

After following the new tunnel for a few hundred feet they reached another tunnel. This one intersected with theirs at a perpendicular angle. This time he felt more confident as he turned right again. The new tunnel was much steeper, with one side heading decidedly deeper into the mountain, while the other one climbed.

Parallel tracks ran along both tunnels. A single iron harp stand lever—so named because the mechanism looked like a harp—nearly five feet high was mounted on two long sleepers. These maneuvered the accompanying linkages to change the direction of the long since disused minecarts.

The new tracks on this tunnel appeared more worn from use and he guessed that this was the main run into the deeper, once highly profitable lower levels of the Queen Charlotte gold mine. Strangely, it was also narrower and the height was low enough that Sam had to keep ducking to stop from hitting his head. Presumably, there was no gold to be found in this section and it was only ever used as a means of bringing the men down into the gold rich depths, and the ore back out again.

Sam's back ached as he carried his equipment hunched over in the shallow tunnel and his mind wandered aimlessly.

Until Sandi interrupted his thoughts.

"Will you continue to head to Colorado Springs?" she asked.

"Not now." Sam shook his head. "This has changed everything. I'll head to Salt Lake City to get a flight to Washington, where my team can get a better understanding of what's going on. You want to join me?"

"Are you kidding?" she said. "Of course, I want a chance to examine it."

"Good. You can provide an alternative theory to the one I have."

"You've seen it before?" Sandi asked.

"Yeah." Sam closed his eyes, as though remembering a recent image from a photograph. "The image I've seen was taken inside a hidden cave, submerged in the South Pacific, and depicted seven similar masks."

"All humanoid?"

"Yes. But only one *Homo sapiens*."

"What were the others of?"

"*Homo erectus, Homo floresiensis, Homo habilis, Homo heidelbergensis, Homo naledi, Homo neanderthalensis.*"

"How bizarre." She paused, remembering the finer details of the mask they'd found inside the obsidian chamber. "If I had to guess, I'd say the mask here comes from a *Homo erectus* — but I might just be guessing that because it would confirm my theory about early migration by *Homo erectus* into North America."

"We'll get out of here and back to Washington where we can run some tests and get a better idea. Also, I'm hoping you might be able to make sense of its connection to the other masks on the pictograph in the ancient cave," Sam said.

"Where did you say the picture was taken?"

"In a submerged cave in the South Pacific."

"Who took the photo?"

"You wouldn't believe me if I told you."

The edge of her lips curled in a wry grin. "Your reputation precedes you, Sam. You're a magician who trades in discoveries of the unbelievable. Try me."

Sam grinned. "Amelia Earhart."

CHAPTER TWELVE

I T TOOK SAM SEVERAL MINUTES to fill Sandi and Jesse in on their discovery of the strange, now submerged island, in the South Pacific, and the discovery of Amelia Earhart's jacket and camera, but no sign of her or her navigator's body.

At the end of the discussion, Sam explained how the photos, presumably from 1937, were developed by historical specialists and that they revealed one particularly strange image of the inside of a large cave, in which a series of seven pictographs showed what appeared to be the last remaining seven sub-species of the family Hominidae.

They passed a couple of old iron mine carts, still on the track, with their brakes in the locked position. A faint light formed at the tunnel's opening.

Sandi opened her mouth, as though she was going to discuss something important about the strange mask, and then asked, "What's that noise?"

Sam listened.

There was a distant high-pitched sound coming from outside the tunnel. He waited as the pitch of the sound changed. It was an engine or possibly two or more, two-stroke engines. Someone had opened its throttle and the motorcycle was racing toward its powerband.

"Motor bikes!" Sam said. "Any chance your local ranger would use a two-stroke?"

"Not a chance in hell," Jesse said. "They might be some kids on dirt bikes having fun."

Sam cocked a worried eyebrow. "You get some of those up here?"

Jesse nodded. "Sometimes in the summer break, but not usually this time of year."

At the entrance to the tunnel a familiar Yamaha YZ250 motorcycle slid to a crisp stop. A second or two later, two identical riders pulled up alongside.

Sam swallowed.

Jesse said, "Now what?"

Sam said, "Now we wait and see if they're a few kids riding motocross for fun... or..."

"They've been sent here to finish what the phony Sam Reilly had begun," Sandi finished for him.

The motocross rider flashed a powerful headlight down into the tunnel. Sam glanced around looking for a side tunnel or crevasse to hide, but there were none. The three of them stood out like animals caught in a powerful spotlight.

The riders revved their engines.

They sounded menacing, if that was even possible for a motorcycle.

And then the first rider took off.

Deeper inside the mine, the tunnel's ceiling dipped and the riders wouldn't be able to keep going, but out here, toward the entrance, the tunnel was somehow taller, allowing the riders to ride in the upright position as the bikes entered the mine and raced toward them.

Sam shouted, "Time to go!"

They started to race back the way they came, deeper into the mountain, running along the narrow-gauge tracks used by the minecart in times long since passed.

Sandi said, "Where?"

"Anywhere but here!" he turned to Jesse. "I don't suppose there's another way out of this mountain?

Jesse grinned. "As a matter of fact, there is."

CHAPTER THIRTEEN

IT WAS IMPOSSIBLE TO OUTRUN a motorcycle on foot.

Up ahead were a pair of twin dilapidating mine-carts. They were roughly seven feet long, by three wide and three high. Made of solid iron, with a total of four railway wheels, the heavy carts were designed to carry more than a ton of gold rich ore.

Sam shouted, "Into the mine cart."

"Oh no!" Sandi shouted, "I'm not getting into that old thing… I'd rather take my chances negotiating with the riders."

Sam shrugged. "Suit yourself."

Leaving the first minecart as a natural shield and impediment to the riders behind, he released the second minecart's brake. He and Jesse started pushing the heavy iron cart down the tunnel, until it picked up speed on its own.

Jesse climbed in first.

Sam kept pushing from behind, gripping the iron holds used by miners from a bygone era when they rode the carts.

He held out his hand for Sandi who was running fast behind. "Quick, give me your hand!"

She looked at him, her face distorted by fear and indecision.

Any doubt about the motocross rider's intentions were shattered a moment later, when the one at the front pulled out a handgun and started to fire directly at them.

The shots slammed helplessly into the ore cart behind them.

That was enough for her. She took his hand and Sam pulled her onto the cart. A moment later she'd climbed inside and took cover.

Jesse said, "You'd better get inside too, Sam. The roof's about to disappear."

Sam's head snapped forward. His eyes locked on the tunnel up ahead where the ceiling of the shaft became not much larger than the minecart itself, as it turned steeply into its downward descent.

He didn't need to be told twice.

Sam climbed over the iron railing and dipped his head, just as the cart disappeared into the darkness of the shallow tunnel.

With the ceiling nearly the same height as the ore cart, they had to keep their heads down inside the cart, or risk losing them altogether. At first Sam had kept his flashlight on, but now there seemed like no point; it wasn't like they could see where they were going.

The cart picked up speed rapidly. Its old wheels made a cacophony of sounds as the metal on metal sent shards of sparks shooting through the velvet darkness of the tunnel like shooting stars. Sam felt the contents of his guts shift as the ore cart turned sharply to the right, before punching out of the corner into an even steeper decline, like a bobsled racing down a luge.

All fear of the attacking riders disappeared.

They raced faster still and for a moment Sam was certain they were about to be thrown out of the uncontrolled ore cart.

"Jesse!" Sam shouted. "How do we slow this damned thing?"

"That lever there," Jesse replied, switching his flashlight on again so that its beam was directed at the mechanism. "But I wouldn't touch it yet."

Sam was just about ready to force his way across the cart and shove the brake lever all the way forward. "Why not?"

"We need the speed."

"We're already going fast!" Sam yelled above the whine of the grinding wheels.

"Not fast enough."

Sandi intervened, "For what?"

"To get up the next rise!"

Sam gritted his teeth and held on. He felt helpless. There was nothing he could do to change the outcome of the events around him, a sensation to which he was highly unaccustomed.

There was no way of telling his speed.

The cart reached a shallow dip that he hadn't noticed on his way up the tunnel earlier, and the ore cart slowed as it reached the crest, like the open car of a roller coaster slowing as it climbed before dipping sharply.

The cart lurched forward, picking up speed quickly.

"How much farther?" Sam asked.

Jesse grinned sardonically. "A fair way. We need to descend a total of eleven hundred feet into the mountain!"

"Eleven hundred feet!" Sam shouted. "Why? I thought you said you knew another way out of the mine!"

"I do."

"So why are we going deeper," Sam asked. "Don't we need to climb?"

"We want the Queen Maud's reef. That shaft runs clear through the mountain, exiting into a state forest."

They passed underneath a small waterfall, with the dripping water hitting them at speed like pellets from a gun.

Sam wiped the water out of his eyes. He looked up. The ceiling seemed more distant, as though the tunnel had suddenly opened up into a wider space. He shined his flashlight on the ceiling, where quartz crystal speckled with fine particles of gold reflected back at him from a height of forty feet at least.

"Where are we?" Sam asked.

Jesse said, "Queen Victoria's Vault."

Sam grimaced. "Where?"

"Queen Victoria's Vault. The largest stope in the region. It was once the richest gold reef in the entire mountain and the miners, God bless them, worked their way through the area like an army of termites, removing every piece of the reef that wasn't absolutely necessary to maintain the structural integrity of the mountain."

Sam said, "Why did they stop? I thought I saw plenty of specks of gold in the quartz."

"You probably did."

"So, what happened?"

"It became unprofitable to extract at the time and nowadays, with modern technology, what's left of the reef would be considered too meagre to go to the trouble of setting up a modern day operation."

"Why?" Sam asked, with surprising curiosity. "Because it's too high up?"

"No." Jesse grinned like an insane devil. "Because it's too far down."

"There's nothing below us?"

"Have a look for yourself," Jesse said cheerfully. "You needn't worry about hitting your head on the roof any longer. From here on in, the old miners took just about every scrap of rock they could get their grubby little hands on and hauled it outside for processing."

Sam sat up, fixing the beam of his flashlight up ahead to make certain that he wasn't about to lose his head on a low overhanging rock. Relieved to see that there was nothing but the darkness of an open vault, he adjusted his position so that he was sitting fully upright. He swept the cathedral-like vault with his flashlight.

So much rockface had been removed he wondered how the entire mountain managed to sustain itself and not collapse.

He didn't let his mind contemplate that risk for very long.

Instead, he aimed his flashlight downward.

The depths of the giant void swallowed the light whole. He maneuvered the beam a little, expecting to see some sort of structure or rockworks, but instead found nothing. Turning to the back of the ore cart he fixed the beam onto the narrow track.

And swore.

Because the hundred plus year old mine tracks now traversed a bridge so high that, despite being able to see through the gaps between the tracks, he couldn't make out the bottom far below.

Sam's jaw clenched shut, his lips thinned. He ran his tongue across the inside of his mouth, as though he'd just tasted something incredibly vile. His heart raced and his chest tightened.

He said, "How much farther?"

"We should be a little over halfway."

The ore cart rose over a gentle ridge and then entered a moderate sized tunnel section of what appeared to be a giant pillar of stone, presumably once left by the miners so as to avoid the collapse of the entire cathedral vault above.

Sam ducked his head instinctively, but he needn't have worried about it. Even within the tunneled pillar, the miners had clawed away as much of the valuable gold rich quartz as they possibly could.

The cart dipped again and descended across another chasm via an almost imperceptible bridge. Sam imagined himself on the worst—or best depending on the way you looked at it— roller coaster ride at Disneyland, with the one difference being that those rides were well engineered and regularly tested. The one he was on now hadn't been used regularly for decades. All it would take was one rotten beam and they were going off the bridge into the dark rift below.

He squeezed his eyes shut and put the thought out of his mind. There was nothing he could do about it anyway.

Sometimes life comes down to luck.

The ore cart entered a relatively horizontal shaft.

Sandi pulled the brake hard. Iron slammed against iron as the brakes screeched along the track. The heavy ore cart barely slowed, putting up a modest fight, until she shoved all her weight into it. The cart finally jolted to a stop.

"What did you do that for?" Jesse asked, his voice harsh.

"I've had enough," she said, climbing out of the ore cart. "I want to get off the ride."

"But we're not there yet!"

"I don't care. I've spent one day with you and already I've nearly died a dozen times. I'm done. I'll walk."

Sam smiled. "Hey, I'm with her. This jittery old cart and the hundred-year-old tracks give me the creeps." Speaking to Jesse, he said, "How much farther do you think we have to go from here?"

Jesse thought about that for a moment. "It's been a while since I came down this far, but at my best recollection, I'd say we're about a half mile off from the Queen Maud reef. Once there, we're about an hour's walk out of the mountain."

Sam looked at Sandi. "What do you think?"

"Half a mile. Ten miles. What difference does it make?" She glanced at the mine cart. "I'd walk a thousand to avoid ever getting back in that thing again."

Sam said, "All right. We walk. It's not like the motocross riders managed to follow us all the way down here. That ceiling, for most of the way, was too low for anyone to ride under. So, I guess we're safe."

Jesse paled. "I wouldn't be so sure."

Sam snapped his flashlight around to the way they had come.

The tunnel was long and straight, allowing them to see as far as the light could reach before it too became overcome by darkness. There was nothing coming.

"I don't see anything," he said.

Sandi's eyes narrowed. "Neither do I."

Jesse swallowed hard. "It doesn't mean they're not coming."

Sam put his hand on the iron track. It was vibrating. There was little more than a tremor, but it was enough to be certain.

He ran his eyes along the track. The entire track seemed to be shaking now. Sam squinted and his ears strained to make sense of the sound.

His eyes went wide at the realization. "The riders must have taken the second ore cart to follow us!"

CHAPTER FOURTEEN

S AM, JESSE, AND SANDI ALL pushed the ore cart, urging it to build up speed. The screeching sound of metal on metal filled the tunnel, as the second ore cart hurtled toward them, causing all three of them to push harder.

"Climb in!" Sam motioned to Sandi, who was by far the lightest among them.

She didn't need to be asked twice this time. She gripped the handle with her right arm and climbed over. "I'm in!"

"You next!" Sam said to Jesse.

Jesse launched himself onto the side railing and climbed in with the supple ease of a much younger man.

"Your turn," Jesse shouted, his voice almost drowned by the screeching of the ore cart's wheels.

Sam reached his peak speed on foot. He lunged forward to grip the hand cart and slipped.

A series of shots fired, echoing in his ears.

He stopped himself from falling to the ground by doing a sort of shuffle with his feet, but his hand missed the cart.

"Let's go Reilly," Jesse said. "They've reached the straight tunnel!"

Sam knew that meant the second cart was still five or six hundred feet away, but now moving along a straight line, with the riders capable of shooting. They would be impossible shots, but anyone can get lucky, or severely unlucky.

It was enough to urge him on.

Sam powered on with his legs, swinging his arms like the pistons of an engine, and he dived for the ore cart.

His right hand gripped the handle and locked on.

Sam's feet started to drag, unable to keep up with the cart's speed. His knuckles turned white, refusing to release his iron hold. His chest burned and the muscles of his legs ached. Jesse gripped his left hand and pulled him in.

Sam took a couple deep breaths. "Thanks."

Jesse said, "Don't thank me too much. I have no idea where we're going to lose them now. We're dead once this ride is over, and I'll end up being the cause of your death after all."

"We're not dead yet," Sam said, defiantly.

"You got a plan?"

"That depends…"

Jesse raised his eyebrows. "On?"

"Whether or not there are any other tunnels offshoots between here and the Queen Maud reef."

"Yes, coming up soon. Only one though. Queen Maud's the end of the line. What were you thinking?"

Sam grinned. "I was thinking if we can reach another switchstand lever, we might divert our unwanted guests."

"Good idea, but we're going to need to slow them down first, or they'll see right through our ruse."

Sandi picked up a couple pieces of quartz ore. "Leave that to me!"

Sam got the idea instantly. They started to pass the rocks

backward where he dumped them onto the track. At the speed they were going, it was unlikely the rocks would cause the pursuing ore cart to derail, but hopefully it might slow them somewhat.

The incoming ore cart was now about a hundred feet behind them. Sam picked up a rock that fit comfortably in the palm of his hand, aimed, and threw it.

With the combined speed of his throw and that of the pursuing cart, the rock managed to reach its target, smashing into a pile of splintered shards on impact. It was a lucky throw but it had done little to hinder the progress of their pursuers.

Sam picked up another stone and tried again.

This one missed completely.

He gripped a third, took aim, and…

Bang!

He heard the shot fire.

It struck the side of his throwing arm, narrowly grazing him.

He swore and yanked his arm back inside the protection of the iron cart.

Examining the wound, he confirmed it was little more than a graze. The throbbing pain was a nagging reminder not to place himself in the direct line of sight of his attackers again.

Instead, they bundled all the rocks into Sam's small backpack. It took a few minutes, and by the time they were done it took all of his strength and willpower to lift the pack over the back of the cart and let it fall.

He glanced back in the dark and watched the sparks fly when the incoming ore cart collided with the stones. It was followed by an awful sound of metal grinding on metal. Sam hoped to hell the damned thing would derail, but instead it seemed to grind to a stop.

Sam heard the voices of men cursing. He tried to see if the cart was permanently disabled, but soon his own ore cart turned a corner, and he lost sight of the wreck.

"Do you think their cart's destroyed?" Sam asked.

Jesse's voice was emphatic. "No way."

"You saw the way those sparks flew?" Sam asked. "They hit the bag pretty hard."

"That iron cart weighs close to a ton. You'd need to hit it with a bus to do any real sort of damage."

Sam grinned. "But we slowed them down, and that's all we need."

The ore cart dipped dramatically, before running across another small bridge that split a large stope in two. At the end of the opening, the track's direction changed abruptly to the left and dipped again, causing Sam to feel as though he'd entered a free fall for a moment, before gravity caught up with them, and the cart was slammed into the gently banking track.

Up ahead, the track split into two.

Sam applied the brake gently, "Which way?"

Jesse said, "Right!"

Sam applied more force to the brake until the ore cart slowed to a crawl as it passed the switchstand lever that rose approximately four feet high beside the track.

Once they passed, he climbed out of the cart and pulled on the lever.

The harp mechanism was a simple lever which pivoted on an axle pin located midway up the main body of the stand. The upper part of the lever passed through a slot atop the stand. As he pulled on the lever, the bar moved the rail into the alternate position.

Certain that the track was now set to go left instead of right, he climbed onto the back of the ore cart. Sandi lifted the brake and the cart started to move again.

The track continued for another few hundred feet before coming to its end in a large vaulted chamber, where four separate tunnels converged. To the right were the remains of an old ore crusher, and a deep dry void that had probably once been used as a sump during the mine's operations.

Sam applied the brake fully into the secure position. It was an automatic habit, but as he climbed out he realized it was an odd thing to do, given they had reached the bottom of the tunnel and would never use it again.

He swept the beam of his flashlight around the room. Each of the converging tunnels were horizontal and without tracks. He imagined the old miners had followed whatever leads they had found, removing the rock and digging deeper in all directions until they no longer found any viable gold reefs.

"Which way?" Sam asked.

Jesse studied each of the tunnels as though he were trying to determine which way to go. Through narrowed eyes, he said, "Can I have a look at your compass."

"Sure." Sam raised his eyebrow and handed him the compass. "You don't know?"

Jesse shrugged. "It's been a long time since I came down this far."

"How long?"

"I was still a boy when my father took me down here... so, at least sixty years."

Sam grimaced. Sixty years was a long time. There could have been plenty of cave-ins, and tunnels may have collapsed or become flooded. Who knows? Sam kept his mouth shut. There was nothing they could do about it now. They would just have to deal with whatever happened.

Sandi said, "What's that?"

Sam flicked his light on the track.

They were shaking again.

"Oh shit!" Jesse cursed. "They didn't buy the ruse."

CHAPTER FIFTEEN

S AM WAS THE FIRST TO recover from the news.

To Jesse, he said, "Which way out?"

Jesse opened his mouth, paused, and said, "That way. To the east."

All three of them ran along the tunnel. It was small, but high enough that none of them had to worry about hitting their heads.

They kept running until their muscles burned with exhaustion. When they couldn't run any farther, they rested by walking briefly, and then kept running.

After nearly an hour in the tunnel, Sam heard the sound of something up ahead. It was hard to determine what it was exactly. Sound travels strangely through a tunnel. Sometimes the narrow confines helped the sound wave bounce from wall to wall, resonating louder as it echoed, but other times, the sound would be lost down a distant tunnel, and you wouldn't hear a thing until you rounded a corner and came face to face with the source of the noise.

"What is that?" Sandi asked.

"I have no idea," Sam said.

His ears locked onto the distant sound as it droned on far down the tunnel. He heard something similar before, but his mind was having trouble identifying it.

To Jesse, he asked, "Where does this tunnel come out?"

"The Pike and San Isabel National Forests and Cimarron and Comanche National Grasslands."

"So there's not likely to be much traffic or machinery noise entering the tunnel."

"No, whatever that sound is, it's coming from inside."

Sam thought about it for a moment. "Any idea how much farther this tunnel runs?"

"Shouldn't be much longer now," Jesse replied. "In fact, I was pretty certain we should have reached the end of the tunnel about twenty minutes ago."

Sam swallowed. "There's a good chance we're in the wrong tunnel, isn't there?"

"Yep."

"All right. Let's keep going. If nothing else, we might find a way to better arm ourselves against our attackers."

Up ahead, in the dark, the distant noise started to resonate louder, until it drowned out their footsteps, and eventually even their voices.

Sam rounded a corner.

The tunnel petered out into a dead end. In its place was the rapid torrent of a flowing waterfall, gushing down on top of them.

CHAPTER SIXTEEN

S AM SHINED THE BEAM OF his flashlight along the waterfall.
There were a series of vertical wooden ladders and their wooden platforms, standing end on end, as they rose to dizzying heights, possibly a hundred or more feet above them. Water fell from the ladders, wooden platforms, and a ventilation shaft before disappearing into an underground siphon, leading deeper into the mountain.

He turned to Jesse. "Wrong place?"

Jesse nodded, apologetically. "Yeah, wrong place."

Sam shot him a thin-lipped smile. "You got any ideas?"

"Not really. I guess it's time we arm ourselves and prepare to face our attackers. There are not a lot of places here to hide."

"I've got an idea," Sandi said.

"Go for it," Sam said.

Sandi shined her flashlight upward. "What about up there?"

Sam swallowed. "You're kidding. That wood looks like it's been down here for a hundred or more years. Do you think it will still take our weight?"

Jesse shrugged as though it didn't really warrant asking. "Might do. Might not."

Sam looked around, thinking if there might have been another option. Then he spotted the flashlight coming from the way they had come.

"Okay, up it is."

CHAPTER SEVENTEEN

S AM CLIMBED THE OLD WOODEN rungs quickly.

Water rushed over his back and his eyes stung, but he made progress. Sandi, as the lightest person, directly behind, with Jesse insisting on climbing last—arguing that he'd gotten everyone into this mess and as a consequence he should be the last to get out.

Sam pressed on, against the downpour.

About seventy feet up, Sam started to feel confident. The rungs were old, but they were taking his weight.

They were nearing the top.

Sam climbed over the last rung and expelled a deep breath. They had made it! It would take a crazy person to try and follow them now.

Over the rumble of the roaring water, he heard the faint sound of several shots being fired, presumably until their attacker's magazine emptied. The sound was immediately followed by a loud cry.

It was a deep guttural, almost visceral, curse.

Sam edged to the side of the wooden platform and looked

down.

Jesse met his eye. "Those bastards hit me!"

"Can you move?"

"Yeah. It just hurts like hell."

Sam waited until Jesse reached his arm and helped pull him up onto the platform.

In a whisper, he said, "Where are you hit?"

"In my butt!"

Sam and Sandi leaned in on either side of him, so that Jesse could use them both for support. Sam had offered to carry him, but Jesse had been insistent it would slow them down too much—although no one believed anyone would willingly climb those ladders if they didn't have to do so.

The ventilation shaft didn't come out on the surface, but instead came out on another horizontal tunnel.

"Great!" Sam said, "I feel like we're trapped in an underground maze."

Sandi said, "More like a minotaur's labyrinth."

In ancient Greek mythology, The Minotaur dwelt at the center of the Labyrinth, which was an elaborate maze-like construction designed by the architect Daedalus and his son Icarus, on the command of King Minos of Crete.

Sam's lips curled into a wry grin. "Trust an anthropologist to make a reference to ancient Greek mythology."

Sandi turned to Jesse. "I don't suppose you know where we are?"

"Actually, I think I know exactly where we are. This one comes out at an abandoned mine in an old ghost town named, St. Elmo's."

"Which way?" Sam asked, noticing there was no light in either direction.

Jesse pointed his flashlight to the left. "That way."

"You're sure?" Sam asked, "Everything is dark."

"I'm sure! I've been exploring these tunnels since I was a kid when my father worked in them. It's a long tunnel and the adit at the entrance has been closed off with timber to stop would-be ghost mine explorers from getting themselves killed."

"All right. Let's just hope we can get out."

Jesse grinned. "We'll get out of here. They haven't yet built the mine that could contain me indefinitely."

They set out at a jogging pace with intermittent five-minute intervals of walking. Jesse expressed significant pain in his gluteus maximus muscles from his wound.

It was nearly another hour before the velvet darkness of the tunnel was torn by the sudden shining of a bright light and the sound of a motorcycle.

Sam pointed his flashlight at a small opening in the side of the tunnel. "Everyone in!"

The motorcycle's two-stroke engine whined as though its rider had suddenly spotted their light. A hunter racing toward its prey.

All three of them switched off their flashlights and clambered into a small excavation in the side of the tunnel. Squatting down inside the alcove, Sam felt something hard and metal. His fingers gripped the handle. He picked up the old miner's tool. It was long, approximately three or four feet, and heavy. Even in the pitch dark, he could the imagine the old pry bar being used to dislodge larger pieces of stone from the crumbling wall.

He gripped it and silently made his way to the very edge of the tunnel. There, he waited, as the motorcycle raced toward him at full speed, its rider oblivious to the peril hiding in wait. It was hardly sharp enough to inflict any real damage on the rider, but maybe it could be used for another purpose.

Sam listened as the rider got closer.

The bike raced by.

Sam drove the iron pry bar through the forks in the front wheel.

The prybar clanged against the fork with a crashing thump as the wheel locked, sending the rider flipping forward.

In the dark it was hard to see the bike flip, and its rider landed with a sickening crunch into the rocky wall of the tunnel. The bike's headlight remained intact, providing a meager amount of ambient light.

Sam moved quickly in the darkness.

With his small dive knife in hand, he moved the blade to the rider's throat, before the rider had time to orient himself again or reach for his weapon.

Sam felt the warm, sticky, liquid cover his hands.

A moment later, Sam removed the knife.

There was no need to guard a dead man.

The rider's un-helmeted face had been smashed by the rock, crushing part of the man's face, killing him instantly.

Sam searched the man and removed his handgun—a Glock 19—checked that its magazine was fully loaded, and prepared to continue on the outward stretch.

"Is he, all right?" Sandi asked, in a voice Sam mistook for panicked concern.

Sam shook his head. "He's dead."

She sighed. "Thank god!"

Sam said, "At least we know that way leads out."

"Let's keep going," Jesse said, indifferently.

But Sam stepped into the alcove again and said, "We're not going anywhere yet."

Because the light of a second rider started to race toward them.

CHAPTER EIGHTEEN

H IDDEN IN THE ALCOVE FOR a second time, Sam waited with the handgun drawn.

He watched as the motorcycle passed and then slowed to a stop twenty or so feet away, its rider dismounting to investigate his comrade.

While the rider squatted down, Sam approached with his Glock drawn. "Hands in the air!"

The rider paused, raised his hands.

Sam asked, "Who sent you?"

The man remained silent.

"Why did you want to hide the mask?" Sam persisted.

Still no response.

"We have the mask and the world will know all about it soon enough, so you'd better start talking."

The rider's eyes widened and the lines in his face deepened.

"Why are you trying to bury it forever?"

Still no response.

"Yeah, well, your plan failed miserably. You failed. The

whole world will know the truth soon."

The man shook his head. "You have no idea what's at stake, do you?"

"With what?" Sam asked.

"We've failed." The man's voice was quiet, barely a coarse whisper, beneath his choked breath. "After centuries, the masks are going to be combined and we will have failed in our task to protect the world."

"Protect the world?" Sam asked. "From what?"

"From them!"

Sam asked. "Who?"

"Those who would like to see an end to all that the Master Builders have created."

Sam's heart raced. What did this man know? "What do you know about the Master Builders?"

Terror filled the man's dark eyes. "They'll kill me for speaking!"

Sam said, "Just wait… we can protect you!"

The man's eyes darted toward the handgun at its holster on his hip.

"No, don't!" Sam yelled. "We can protect you."

The man shook his head, his eyes wide and possessed with fear. "You can't even save yourselves anymore. No one can!"

The rider reached for his pistol.

Sam fired first.

Two shots.

They hit the man in his chest.

The rider fell backward. Then, seemingly uninjured behind a bulletproof vest, sat up, gripped his own handgun, pointed the barrel to the bottom of his throat and pulled the trigger.

The bullet took off his jaw, ripping a hole through the man's brainstem, killing him instantly.

Sam stood up. He pocketed the man's weapon—a Sig Sauer P226—and started the motorcycle.

"Now we can go!"

Sandi opened her mouth to speak, but words didn't come out.

Sam said, "What?"

Her eyes widened, "You've been shot!"

Sam looked down.

Blood flowed freely from what appeared to be a single gunshot wound.

CHAPTER NINETEEN

"**R**ELAX!" SAM SAID. "I'M NOT shot."

Sandi shook her head. "That's shock answering there. No. You've been hit."

Sam grinned. His words, emphatic, "No, I haven't."

"You haven't?"

"Not today anyway. I just tore open an old wound."

"How old?"

"Three weeks."

"You were shot three weeks ago?"

Sam nodded, giving a little shrug. "Like I said, sometimes my work can be a touch dangerous."

"One day you'll have to explain to me why people like to keep shooting at an oceanographer."

"Hey, I'd like to know the answer to that, too." Sam helped Sandi pick up the motorcycle. "You can ride?"

She climbed on and started the engine, revving the throttle a little. "Of course I can ride a bike!"

"Good, because there's no way Jesse's in any position to ride on his own. He can ride pillion with me."

A minute later, Sandi followed after Sam as he drove first along the tunnel.

Up ahead, another man on a dirt bike slowed to meet them. In the blinding beam of his headlight, the rider hadn't realized it was Sam.

The biker yelled, "Any sign of them?"

Sam aimed the Sig Sauer and squeezed the trigger. At six feet away, the man didn't have a chance. The single shot went right through the center of the guy's chest, killing him.

Sam said, "That's for running me off the road!"

He kicked the bike into gear, released the clutch and continued riding.

The horizontal mine tunnel opened up into the inside back of an old dilapidated building in St. Elmo's. It looked like the place was being used by gold prospectors to illegally access the old mine site.

He aimed the bike toward the front door and revved the throttle, which lifted the front wheel up just a notch, and rode through the door—sending it splintering into a thousand shards of broken wood.

An hour later they were at the sheriff's department back at Nathrop. Betty was already there, and so was an ambulance to take Jesse to the hospital. The paramedics wanted to look at Sam's head injury, but he brushed it aside. After all, it had been nearly twelve hours since he'd had the accident.

One of the sheriff's deputies asked Sam and Sandi to wait there for a few hours while their officers searched the mine site for their attackers.

They agreed.

Sandi said to Sam, "You know there's going to be hell to pay because of the high body count that we racked up."

Sam shrugged. "Better them than us."

CHAPTER TWENTY

BY THAT EVENING A MAN in his early forties turned up in a sheriff's uniform.

The man said, "My name's Jeff Mills. I'm in charge in this neck of the woods."

Sam stood up to shake the man's hand. "Sam Reilly. Pleased to meet you, sir. This is Professor Sandi Larson."

Jeff glanced at them both. He smiled apologetically. "I'm really sorry you've had such a lousy time out here. But I'm glad you pulled through."

"Did you find the riders who attacked us?"

"Afraid not."

"What about the driver of the Porsche? Sandi gave his description to one of your deputies earlier."

"No luck there, I'm afraid."

Sam leveled his eyes at the sheriff. "What do you know?"

Jeff met his eye. "I don't know what to tell you. We've sent a team into the mine shaft that ran through the old post office at St. Elmo's. It looks like the tunnel had been in existence since the

1920s when the gold mine was in full swing. But we haven't found any evidence of a group of riders searching for some mask."

Sandi asked, "What about the bodies?"

"I don't know what to say, ma'am. We didn't find any bodies."

Her eyes narrowed. "You searched the mine?"

"Yeah, we searched the mine. All the way to the end. There's nothing there."

"Can you get surveillance of the area?"

"I've tried. There's nothing on it. So what do you suggest I do?"

Sam grinned. "Well, sir. You've had someone attempt to commit the murder of three people by intentionally detonating the entrance to the Queen Maggie mine shaft in order to conceal an old artifact. Rick Rodier, an archeologist from the University of Chicago, was shot and killed. In addition to that, I shot three people in self-defense and now those bodies have been removed—professionally and quickly by the sound of it."

The sheriff nodded. "Again, what do you suggest I do?"

Sam sighed. "Well, sir. I'd put your report together, making sure you dot your I's and cross your T's. Then I'd contact the FBI, because one thing's for certain, this extends well out of your local jurisdiction."

The sheriff crossed his arms. "Without any bodies, what do you expect me to do?"

"Open an investigation?"

"Without any bodies, why should I go chasing ghosts in a disused mine?"

CHAPTER TWENTY-ONE

Denver International Airport

S AM WAITED AT THE AIRPORT for a flight to Washington, D.C. Tom Bower, his best friend, and diving companion, had driven up from Colorado Springs to meet him there, along with his girlfriend, Genevieve Callaghan. Sam put Sandi Larson on a flight to Heathrow, London, with the strange mask. She said that she could have a better explanation for what the mask was within a day or two, as well as providing a reasonable estimate of its age. Sam insisted on sending Genevieve to protect her and guard the mask until they knew better what it was they were dealing with. When Sandi complained that she'd feel safer with him around, Sam pointed out that Genevieve was one of the most lethal persons alive. In the end, Sandi had acquiesced.

After leaving the two girls at the gate, Sam and Tom sat down to eat a late dinner. It was a takeaway burger joint. Nothing special, but it hit the spot.

Tom said, "Some vacation?"

Sam nodded. "Yeah. I'm calling it about par for the course."

Tom grimaced. "That bad, huh…"

"Yeah."

"How was the Lamborghini?"

Sam's lips curled with joy. "It's beautiful. I mean. It's a Lamborghini… so what am I supposed to say, it sucks? But really, it was a work of art in its day. They took a risk to produce the most formidable bomb-proof four-wheel drive cum race car, back in a time well before the SUV market had begun."

"Nice. How was Aliana?"

Sam smiled. He and Aliana dated a number of years ago, before she broke it off with him because of his reckless lifestyle. A few weeks ago, their lives had been serendipitously smashed together again. As it was, he owed her a trip to a warm deserted island in the Pacific. Instead, she got a four-wheel driving trip in Moab, Utah.

He couldn't answer for himself where they were, but it was nice to spend a couple days with her again. Maybe next time he'd take her to Tahiti. He met Tom's prying gaze. "It was nice."

"Good for you," Tom said, knowing when to leave it alone.

Sam stood up. "Shall we go find some coffee?"

"Sounds good."

A man took a seat next to them without ordering anything.

Tom, always protective of Sam, glared at the man as though he might be another attacker.

The stranger ignored him, turning to Sam instead. "Sam Reilly?"

Sam studied the man at a glance.

The stranger was wearing a suit and tie. His hands were clean. He wore glasses and looked more like an office worker than a hitman. Besides, if he worked for whoever had tried to get him killed, the man wouldn't have made his move right here — in the middle of the security department of an international airport.

"Yes," Sam replied, offering his hand. "Can I help you?"

The man took it with a surprisingly firm grip. "Gerry Emple."

Sam arched his eyebrow. "I'm sorry have we met?"

"No. I work for the NTSB Air Crash Investigations." The man showed him his credentials. "Any chance we can talk?"

Sam glanced at his watch. It was 8:30 pm. He had an hour to kill before his flight. "Sure. You mind if I get a coffee?"

"No problem."

"Tom wants some coffee, too."

"Not a problem. It's my shout. He might be able to help, too."

"Okay, it's a deal."

Sam and Tom followed him through the security screening section and stopped at a coffee shop in the departures lounge.

He took a seat. This time of the night there weren't many customers.

Sam smiled. "So what's this about?"

Gerry said, "I need your help."

"To do what?"

"I was told you can find things."

Sam grinned. "You're going to need to be a little more specific. What exactly is it that you're missing?"

"An aircraft."

"Big or small?"

"An A380's crashed. We need someone with your expertise to help locate it."

Sam's smile disappeared. He shook his head. "Christ! A second A380 in a matter of months. Two of the safest aircrafts in the world. It's going to cripple the aviation industry."

"No. Just the one. Phoenix flight 318."

The muscles in Sam's face hardened. "I thought you found that three months ago? There were no survivors."

"We just pulled it up from the seafloor. The entire wreck was staged."

"I thought you found the wreckage three days after it disappeared?" Sam shook his head. "It had intentionally weaved its way throughout a series of radar towers and avoided detection, only to eventually run out of fuel and ditch straight into the Mediterranean Sea."

Gerry looked at him like he didn't know what to say, so kept his mouth shut.

Sam continued. "You even released footage from outside the wreck. You sent an ROV down there and found bodies."

"We did."

Sam took a sip of his coffee. "So you've got the right aircraft?"

"Only one problem."

Sam put his coffee down on the table. "What happened?"

"We brought up all of the bodies."

"And?"

Gerry swallowed. "None of them belonged onboard Phoenix Flight 318."

CHAPTER TWENTY-TWO

S AM WAS WORKING HARD TO suppress a grin.

It's hard to steal any aircraft, let alone an Airbus A380, one of the largest and most technologically advanced commercial passenger jets in existence. Then, to make the world believe that the wreckage had been found, only to discover on autopsy that none of the bodies belonged on that flight?

Well, that was nothing short of magic.

The airline industry had gone to great lengths to ensure large commercial aircraft didn't just simply disappear. Sam had never flown large aircraft. Most of his training and experience was with helicopters, starting in the US Navy. But he had a basic understanding of the process for monitoring airspace. The standard practice used two radar systems, primary and secondary. Primary radar detected and measured an estimate of a plane's position using reflected radio signals. Secondary radar relied on targets equipped with a transponder that asks for the plane's identity and altitude. All commercial airlines have a transponder, which automatically sends a transmission with a unique four-digit code when it receives a radio signal sent by radar. This is the data sent to air traffic controllers, who monitor the airspace.

When traveling over the ocean, there is no radar coverage more than a hundred miles away from land. When flying overseas, pilots switch to a high frequency (HF) radio for long-range communication. Commercial pilots are then required to check in at fixed location points through what is called "oceanic communications."

Most modern passenger planes are equipped with a flight management computer known as an FMC that automatically makes a transmission report with the plane's speed, altitude and position at specific points throughout the flight. The pilots then connect the autopilot to the route programmed in the FMC and the airplane will follow the programmed course and make check-ins at fixed location points. Of course, to disguise this, all someone would have to do is simply switch off the FMC and change their direction.

In addition to the FMC transponder, most aircraft have an ADS-B: automatic dependent surveillance broadcast—which provides a data downlink containing various flight parameters to air traffic control systems. The transponder broadcasts on 1090 MHz and other aircraft in the vicinity receive those data as well. Using the aircraft's latitude, longitude, course direction and altitude, complex computers at Oceanic Tracking Stations can produce a radar-like display of the aircraft.

What surprises most people, even today, is that although all large commercial planes are equipped with GPS to track their location, it only lets the crew know where the plane is, not the air traffic controllers, whose network is almost entirely radar-based. If a plane goes off course over the ocean, there isn't any way for air traffic control to know its exact location.

Sam exchanged glances with Tom, trying to gauge his reaction, but his friend's expression was customarily opaque.

His eyes returned to Gerry, and he asked, "You want to tell me what you know so far, from the beginning?"

Gerry opened up a small folder, laying it out on the table.

"Phoenix Flight 318 departed La Guardia International nearly three months ago enroute to Marco Polo International Airport in Venice. It departed on time at 6:55 p.m. New York time. They were designated a standard NAT-OTS." Gerry looked up at Sam and Tom. "I assume you know what that is?"

Sam nodded. "The North Atlantic Organized Track System."

It was a structured set of transatlantic flight routes that stretch from the northeast part of North America to western Europe across the Atlantic Ocean. They ensured aircraft were separated over the ocean, where there is little radar coverage. These heavily traveled routes are used by aircraft traveling between the two continents, flying between the altitudes of 29,000 and 41,000 feet inclusive. Entrance and movement along these tracks were controlled by special Oceanic Control Centers, whose controllers maintained separation between airplanes

Gerry continued. "The flight was supposed to have taken just eight hours and fifteen minutes, meaning they should have landed at Marco Polo at 9:05 a.m."

"That's right," Sam confirmed. "Its ADSB transponder was picked up by the Oceanic Tracking station in Portugal at 07:45, following it up until it disappeared — presumably into the Mediterranean Sea at 08:01."

"Where was that, specifically?" Tom asked.

"It went down in the Ionian Sea." Gerry looked up from his notes and met Sam's eye. "You know what that means, don't you?"

"Phoenix flight 318 disappeared into the Calypso Deep?"

"Exactly. Most of the Mediterranean Sea has an average depth of 4,900 feet, and the deepest point on record is the Calypso Deep at 17,280 feet. Whoever we're dealing with here, knew that and so they placed the counterfeit A380 wreck there, where they knew it was going to be difficult to retrieve the bodies."

"That explains the delay and difficulty retrieving the black box from the wreckage. Impossible to dive at that depth. It would have taken a month to locate an available deep-water submarine capable of making the dive, and setting up a team of ROVs to enter the wreckage."

"Nearly two months by the time we had a full team ready to make the dive."

Sam licked his dry lips. "What did your crew find inside?"

"Everything we expected to find. Dead bodies still in their seats, flight attendants, personal effects and luggage. But it was all a show. Everyone who was down there had been dead a long time."

Sam nodded. "What about the black box?"

"They found it."

"And?"

"At first we thought we'd found everything. It depicted a pilot intentionally alternating from his set course, and then setting the aircraft into an intentional water landing."

"You mean, it was the right aircraft?"

"That's what we thought, but we were wrong. Everything was faked."

"How did you pick that up?"

"First the clouds in the cockpit's video recording didn't match the aircraft at all. They were high forming, cumulus clouds."

"And on the day of the crash?"

"A thick thunderstorm pummeled the entire region, while at cruising altitude there was nothing but dense cloud cover."

"Could it have crashed on another day?" Sam asked.

"No way. If it had, where had it been for the past three days?"

"Right." Sam asked, "What about the passports?"

Gerry made a half-shrug. "The passports were real. So were the bodies. But they didn't match. Our best bet is the deceased stopped breathing years before the aircraft went down."

Sam's eyes narrowed. "Someone went to the trouble of

exhuming an entire aircraft worth of corpses and dumping a new aircraft just to send you down the wrong path? What about the passports?"

"The passports were real though, which means someone on board must know where the old aircraft disappeared."

Sam picked up a piece of paper which displayed the predicted flight path. "You said the Phoenix flight 318 — the real one — was identified by local air traffic control towers and radar as having entered the Mediterranean airspace?"

"That's right. Its onboard transponder showed it cruising in past Madrid at 07.15. It was then picked up by radar stations throughout the Mediterranean Sea, including radar towers at Roma, Barcelona, and Malta."

That caught Sam's attention. "Radar towers got a good image of the aircraft as it flew through the area, crashing into the sea?"

"Yeah... sort of." Gerry's voice faded, like someone who knew his answers wouldn't hold up against public or scientific scrutiny.

"What exactly do you have?"

"Multiple air traffic control towers noted the presence of Phoenix flight 318's transponder as they tracked it through their region."

"Any visuals of the aircraft?"

Gerry shook his head. "No. It was severely overcast on the day, with violent thunder storms raging throughout the region."

"What about the primary radar?"

"It tracked an aircraft flying through the route. It was a deviated course, but nothing that threatened harm or conflicted with any of the authorized flight plans, so no one took any notice until it was too late."

"Deviated... why?"

"Well, Sam. In retrospect, and if I had to guess, I'd say the pilots appear to have taken a very specific route that was most difficult to track with radar."

Sam's eyes narrowed. "What can you say, unequivocally, was tracked by radar?"

"An aircraft displaying the same unique transponder code as Phoenix 318, relaying the same information one would expect from the A380, and traveling a similar course, was picked up roughly a hundred miles out from Portugal—and then tracked as it flew on a course that overshot Madrid, commenced its descent, and eventually crashed into the Ionian Sea at 08:01." Gerry's mouth squirmed as though he'd tasted something bitter. "Why? What are you thinking?"

Sam expelled a deep breath. "I don't think you lost the real Phoenix 318 anywhere near the Ionian Sea. In fact, I doubt the Phoenix even crossed the Atlantic."

Gerry crossed his arms. "You don't? Then what plane did we track?"

"I have no idea, but I intend to find out."

CHAPTER TWENTY-THREE

NTSB Field Office–Catania, Sicily

I T WAS LATE AT NIGHT and cold by the time Sam and Tom, accompanied by Gerry Emple, got off the NTSB jet and made their way to the field office.

The NTSB field office was set up in a large aircraft hangar they had hired from the Catania airport. Sam took in the hangar at a glance. Despite being nearly 11 p.m. a not so small hive of men and women dedicated to getting to the bottom of the strange mystery swarmed the building. At the southern end of the hangar the wreckage of the fake Phoenix Airlines A380 which had been meticulously brought up from the Ionian Sea, now rested on a series of purpose-built frames in three separate pieces. A small army of engineers, forensic scientists, and FBI agents surrounded the wreckage searching for clues as to where it had come from, how it got to the crash site, and who had constructed it.

The problem was, few things survived very well at a depth of 17,280 feet.

There was no longer any doubt about the aircraft being counterfeit. The hull itself was made out of a thin layer of steel, the interior a clever work of art, but the engines had been taken from a disused 747 engine cowling, repainted with the markings of a Rolls Royce Trent 900. By the time investigators stripped the internal panels, they discovered that the entire aircraft was devoid of any wiring. It at least explained how someone managed to steal an A380 to dump in the sea — they didn't.

To the north were walls upon walls of computer charts, digital and real maps, live satellite feeds from the day of the event, and small military attaché from the Sicilian, Italian, Maltese, Nigerian, Spanish, and Portuguese Navies, who were providing additional information about the tracked flight path, weather, and conditions of the Mediterranean Sea during the day of the disappearance.

Gerry introduced them to the lead investigator, Mykel Densley who began bringing them up to speed on the investigation. Sam shook the man's hand. He was tall and wiry, with an expressionless face that exuded high intelligence, with either low social skills, or more likely an indifference to them. The man was an MIT graduate and had a mind like a computer.

Without preamble, Mykel said, "The fake aircraft was put together from spare airplane parts, and a purpose built steel tube to make the fuselage."

Sam asked, "Any idea where the fuselage was constructed? I mean, someone's going to remember building something like that. If it was built out of steel, there's no way anyone would have expected it to fly."

"No. We have two theories. One, that the steel fabricators were informed that the fuselage was intended for another purpose, say, an aviation themed restaurant or motel. The second idea was that whoever's responsible for this, manufactured the entire fuselage themselves."

Tom weighed in on the idea. "It takes a fair amount of technical know-how to construct something this big out of steel."

Mykel steepled his fingers and set his jaw firmly, with what might be construed as arrogance, or certainty. "It takes a lot of know-how to pull off exhuming bodies, setting up the interior décor to pass the first impression by ROVs, not to mention fooling all of us by making us believe we were all tracking the Phoenix flight 318's transponder." He took a deep breath. "Yeah, I think it's fairly safe to say that whoever is responsible for this, they have a reasonable amount of know-how as well as the financial and technical resources to pull it off."

Sam spread his hands to cut him short. "Okay, we get the idea. So how did someone get the wreck here in the first place?"

"By boat. An old ocean liner to be exact. The *T/S Raffaello*." Mykel brought up an image of the vessel.

Sam's eyes widened. "You've impounded the ship?"

"Not yet."

"Why not?"

Mykel tilted his head to the side and grinned. "Well, for a start, the *T/S Raffaelo* sank in 1983."

"Which means the ship was intentionally disguised."

"Right."

"Still, you must be able to find a large ocean liner that meets that description. Where did it go after the Phoenix disappeared?"

"It was last seen leaving the Strait of Gibraltar twelve hours after the Phoenix went missing."

Sam said, "If we can find the crew of that ship, we can get answers."

"That might be difficult. The ship hasn't been seen since."

Sam said, "I have someone who can run an Artificial Intelligence search program over the thousands of satellite photos taken on the day the Phoenix disappeared, as well as since then. It shouldn't be long and we'll find that ship."

"All right," Mykel agreed. "I'm told you're somewhat of an expert in locating lost ships. If you're happy, we'll leave that task to you."

"No problem," Sam replied. "Great, so now we're looking for a ship and an aircraft."

Tom smiled. "Hey, look on the bright side, now we have two needles in the haystack we've doubled our chances of locating one of them."

Sam grinned at Tom's joke. Turning to Mykel he asked, "What about the second aircraft? Do we know where that went?"

Mykel looked blank. "What second aircraft?"

Sam filled him in on his theory about a smaller aircraft, transmitting the Phoenix Flight 318's transponder and security code. It even followed an exact route that made it impossible for any of the radar towers to get a good fix. Then, after transmitting flight data that suggested the aircraft went into a dive and crashed into the Ionian Sea, the pilot simply switched off his transmitter, changed course and speed, and flew out of the airspace above the Mediterranean Sea.

Mykel listened to the whole thing. When Sam had finished, he said, "Good God. You're right! We need to make a list of every aircraft that flew in or out of that airspace on the day."

"You have someone who can do that?" Sam asked.

"Yes of course. I'll get my people on it."

Sam arched his eyebrows. "If I'm right, you know what this means?"

Mykel sighed heavily. "Yes. It means that Phoenix Airlines flight 318 never entered the Mediterranean Airspace… or for that matter, crossed the Atlantic!"

CHAPTER TWENTY-FOUR

S AM AND TOM SPENT THE next four days pouring over satellite images of the Mediterranean Sea on the day the Phoenix disappeared. Elise, Sam's computer whiz and hacker, had provided them with a list of all ship's that passed the Strait of Gibraltar from the week before through to the week after the event.

On the day the Phoenix disappeared, the entire region was shrouded in dense clouds, like a cloak of darkness, which hid the movements of all maritime vessels. Assuming that the ship entered the Mediterranean Sea sometime in the week before the event, there were potentially thousands upon thousands of vessels to search. They cut the thousands of ships down into a list of hundreds, based on the size. No matter which way you looked at it, a vessel capable of bringing in something the size of an A380 — even in three separate pieces — was going to have to be big.

That pretty much left them with cargo ships.

Sam inputted the dimensions of the aircraft into the computer. An A380 was 240 feet long, with a wingspan of 262 feet. The AI program that Elise had designed, utilized images of all known vessels within the area during the time of the Phoenix crash.

Elise called up. "I have an idea."

"Shoot. I'm open to suggestions."

"What if they dropped the aircraft a month earlier?

Sam said, "I don't understand… there was debris and flotsam — oil, luggage, lifejackets from the Phoenix on the sea's surface."

"And all of that was placed there — possibly even by the aircraft that carried the fake transponder."

Sam closed his eyes, trying to picture how he would have done it if he were trying to pull off such an extraordinary hoax. He opened them again, the hint of a smile on his lips. "You're suggesting the counterfeit Phoenix aircraft was dumped there, weeks if not months earlier?"

"That's right. They knew it would be difficult to hide anything on the day of the event, with the waterways packed with search and rescue vessels, navy ships, and aircraft."

"So they sunk the largest part earlier, and then sailed out of the region so that the ship wouldn't be connected to it."

Sam inserted the new parameters into the program and pressed enter. The program ran for twenty-five minutes and stopped.

The results, just one vessel. The *T/S Raffaello*.

During a period of thick fog, the captain had the ship painted another color and transformed into a standard cargo ship. On the deck it showed its true name in bold lettering six feet high — *San Juan*.

Sam handed the printed photo of the *San Juan* to Gerry Emple and said, "I want that image distributed to every marina, coast guard, and navy in the world. Someone's seen it. Someone's going to know where it went. That's our ship. Find that ship, and we'll find out where the Phoenix is."

Two hours later Sam got a phone call. He listened for a couple seconds and then hung up. A second later, he swore vehemently.

Tom asked, "What's wrong?"

"Someone sunk the *San Juan* an hour ago."

"Where?"

"Somewhere in the Tyrrhenian Sea."

"Shit!" Tom cursed. "Most of the Tyrrhenian Sea is deeper than 4,000 feet—much too deep for any useful recovery. Do you know where exactly?"

"Near the Island of Capri… the Italian Navy tried to intercept before they got into the deeper water. In the end the crew sank the *San Juan* off the coast of Capri before a Navy team could board."

"Where exactly?"

"South of Capri."

Tom stood up, his voice rising, "How deep?"

Sam grinned. "A hundred and thirty feet!"

CHAPTER TWENTY-FIVE

Off the Coast of the Island of Capri, Italy

THE *MOONLIGHT SONATA*, A 190-FOOT luxury pleasure cruiser reduced its engines to idle, and coasted along the shallow waters off the Island of Capri. The royal blue of the deep water turned azure and emerald green in these shallows, against the backdrop of vertical walls of white limestone that dominated the island's coastline.

At the helm, Pauline Faller adeptly eased the twin throttle controls back until the vessel came to a standstill in the calm waters.

Sam smiled as he met her eye.

At five foot ten, she had a toned and athletic figure. Her smile was big and commanding, her wit like a wasp, and her mind, razor sharp. Beneath her carefree exterior, there was a hardness, a pain from her past that had been suppressed to the point that it may never be released.

They had met in Afghanistan in 2003, where she had flown fighter jets for the US Air Force. The two of them even dated for a short while after she completed her tour of duty and had moved back stateside. But their lives were headed in different directions. She had seen more combat action than any other pilot since Vietnam. Driven by duty and honor, she achieved some of the highest accolades of any pilot in the past two decades.

But it had come at a price.

PTSD was still considered a dirty word, heavily stigmatized as weakness. She'd gone through her entire career proving that she was hard enough, capable enough, and strong enough to engage in a predominantly male dominated profession. There was no way she was going to turn her back against that now and ask for help. Instead she had become withdrawn and isolated from her friends and family. In the end, she knew that if she didn't do something, she was going to end up paying for it with her life.

So, she resigned her Commission, and just like that, left the old world behind and everything in it—that world included Sam Reilly. It turned out, after years of travel, she finally found a place to call home. She landed a job skippering a luxury motor yacht out of Nice in the French Riviera. The owner, a wealthy businessman, used the yacht with his family a couple weeks a year. She lived aboard and maintained the vessel, but for the rest of the time, she was free to do what she wanted with the vessel.

Sam noted the vagabond lifestyle had agreed with her. It had been ten years since she had broken up with him. Her lithe body was slightly fuller somehow, yet all those curves had managed to fall in just the right places. The sight teased him with a small pang of, *what could have been* if things hadn't ended as they had. Those years had been kind to her. If anything, age had made her more attractive. It made him wonder if she was seeing anyone.

Pauline met his eye, a grin forming on her lips, and for a moment he wondered if she had read exactly what he was thinking of from his face.

He turned and spotted a helicopter circling overhead. It hovered and then landed on the sand off *Cala Grande Beach*, not far from the *Blue Grotto*.

He had dived the *Blue Grotto* years ago.

There, sunlight passed through an underwater cavity and shined through the seawater, creating a blue reflection that illuminated the cavern. The grotto extended some hundred and fifty feet into the cliff, and was nearly five hundred feet deep. During Roman times, the grotto was used as the personal swimming hole of Emperor Tiberius, as well as a marine temple.

At the back of the main cave of the Blue Grotto, three connecting passageways lead to the Sala dei Nomi, or "Room of Names," so-called because of the graffiti signatures left by visitors over the centuries. Two more passages led deeper into the cliffs on the side of island. It was thought that these passages were ancient stairways that led to Emperor Tiberius' palace. However, the passages were natural and despite Sam Reilly being brought in to investigate any below the waterline, all the passages eventually narrowed into a dead end.

Pauline pressed the anchor button, and the Danforth anchor lowered.

Sam said, "It looks like my friends have arrived."

Pauline said, "Take the runabout to pick them up."

"Okay, thanks."

Sam lowered the little motorboat into the water and motored it up to the beach. Matthew, Veyron, and Elise got off the beach and climbed aboard, carrying a heap of diving equipment. A few minutes later he returned to the *Moonlight Sonata* and everyone quickly climbed up.

"Welcome aboard," Sam said. His eyes turned to Pauline, he said, "This is Pauline. We go back to our time in Service with the Armed Forces. She's graciously offered the loan of her vessel while we dive the *San Juan*."

Pauline greeted them with a smile. "Technically, this is my boss's yacht. But he's in Singapore right now, and I'm sure he would approve of using his vessel for a good cause."

Sam introduced them all to her.

"Matthew has worked on my dad's ships for more than thirty years and he and I have worked closely together for more than a decade now. He's skippered every ship I've worked on until recently, when he lost the *Maria Helena*."

Pauline's eyes narrowed on Matthew. "You sunk the *Maria Helena*? That was careless of you. What went wrong?"

Matthew spread his hands. "A rogue submarine fired torpedoes at us."

Pauline opened her mouth, releasing the smallest of laughs, before her eyes landed on Matthew's hardened demeanor, and she said, "Holy shit, you're serious."

Matthew nodded. "Afraid so."

Sam continued. "This is Veyron—no relation to the car. He's an expert engineering Rockstar, specializing in submersibles and ROVs."

"Pleased to meet you, ma'am," Veyron said.

Elise was the last to step on board.

She was slightly shorter than the average American woman, but not by much more than a few inches. She wore cargo shorts and a white tank top, revealing toned and muscular arms. She had golden skin, light brown hair, and a wondrous expression, like life was all one big game, and she was the one with the most talent.

Elise carried a watertight backpack with her laptop and satellite phone. "I'm Elise," she said, offering her outstretched hand.

Pauline took it with a firm shake. "Pleased to meet you. What do you do for Sam?"

"My expertise is in computers. Anything from data mining, high tech communications, through to hacking. I've spent a lot of time developing AI programs for search and rescue."

"I know of numerous uses for AI all over the world, but I've never heard of AI being used in search and rescue. Is it useful?"

"Yes. Very. Think about it. We currently have 1,886 artificial satellites orbiting the Earth," Elise said, using the current statistics correct as of forty-eight hours ago. "That number's rising rapidly, which means we're gathering unimaginable visual images of the globe. When there's a disaster, for example, a ship lost at sea, a commercial aircraft missing, or a tsunami that's washed people out to sea, many of the private companies that own these satellites release hundreds of thousands of images."

Pauline blinked against the strong sunlight reflecting off the nearby beach. "I think I recall hearing something about a sailor going missing in 2017 on an around the world solo sail. They said something about placing the photographs on a website and that way people from all around the world could use it to search for him in the Atlantic Ocean."

"That's right." Elise smiled, revealing a nice set of teeth. "Somewhere on those images, there is almost a certainty, that the missing person or vessel, had been captured by digital camera. The problem is, it might take weeks, months, or even years — assuming they ever are found — to be spotted by human eyes."

"Your AI system is scanning them all?"

"That's right. The images can be fed into the system, and the AI program, designed to search for a particular shape or constellation of shapes, determines which images are most likely to match up with what we're searching for. The program itself is pretty basic, but what AI can do with it is invaluable, yet terrifying and startling at the same time."

Pauline's eyes narrowed. "Why?"

"The AI program can extrapolate enormous amounts of information from very little data, things that no human could possibly achieve."

"Such as?"

"Say you're looking for a plane that went down in the ocean. My system can simultaneously look at hundreds of thousands of images, and by picking up the movement of flotsam, debris, and other floating materials, it could extrapolate where an object floating in the Atlantic Ocean might have originated."

"You're saying we find a wing in the Atlantic Ocean, but your AI program can tell us that the wing most likely came off a plane that crashed in the Southern Ocean?"

Elise nodded. "That's right. Something just like that."

Pauline placed her hands akimbo. "So what's the down side?"

"What?"

"You said that's the benefit of AI in search and rescue, so what's the downside?"

Elise made a dramatic sigh. "Well, like all technology, it could be used for good or evil. Depending on what the user was trying to achieve, it could be used to locate individual people to spy, track, or locate them anywhere in the world. Thus, we're opening a Pandora's Box of privacy problems. Think about it. Say you're in trouble, your life's at stake, and you've entered a witness protection program and moved overseas. Well, given this sort of AI technology, theoretically, someone could locate you anywhere in the world."

"Can they actually do that?"

"It would be hard. The person of interest would need to be outside at the time, without a hat on their head, or looking up at the sky when the satellites came overhead, but yes, with current AI technology, it's possible. You have to remember, it might not locate them on the first run, but the satellites circle the Earth more than twice every twenty-four hours. If they don't capture him today, there's always tomorrow, or the next. Either way, eventually, a person of interest will be found."

"Scary stuff," Pauline said. "So why hasn't it located the Phoenix?"

Elise held her gaze with defiance. "It's not perfect. There's nothing it can do if cloud covers vital pieces of the puzzle. Even so…" her voice faded.

Pauline said, "What?"

Elise smiled. "Even so, I have another theory."

"What's that?"

"I think my AI system hasn't located the wreckage of Phoenix Flight 318, because the aircraft never crashed — or certainly didn't in any ocean throughout the world."

Veyron and Matthew loaded the last crate onto the deck.

Pauline scanned what amounted to nearly a ton of equipment. "What is all that stuff?"

"Mostly dive gear."

She arched an eyebrow. "And?"

Veyron unlatched the watertight locks, and opened a gray case. Inside was a pair of M2 Browning Heavy Machineguns and five Israeli made open-bolt, blowback-operated, Uzis.

Pauline frowned. "Good God! What are they for?"

Sam turned to pacify her. "Whoever's responsible for whatever's going on, has gone to great lengths to cover up the loss of the Phoenix, including exhuming more than four hundred bodies, and faking a massive air crash. They went to the trouble of scuttling the *San Juan* before a Navy ship could intercept it. That means whatever's on board incriminates them with this operation. I have no doubt they're willing to kill to protect it."

Tom said, "I still don't know what they could possibly have left behind down there that they're so worried would lead us to the Phoenix?"

Elise grinned. "How about an AIS beacon?"

AIS stood for automated identification system.

Tom laughed. "You're right. They could have turned off their system, but inside, it would still register its position. Find its unique tracking identifier and we can locate where the ship's been since the day it was first launched."

CHAPTER TWENTY-SIX

T HE *MOONLIGHT SONATA* MOTORED SLOWLY away from the Italian island of Capri, coming to a stop roughly five hundred feet to the south. The graphic display of the depth sounder depicted the clear outline of the large cargo ship of the *San Juan* resting on the seabed some 130 feet below.

Tom spotted the image and grinned. "In an area with an average depth in excess of four thousand feet, they sure messed up when they scuttled the ship in just one-hundred and thirty!"

Sam nodded. "Yeah, according to the attaché from the Italian Navy, they were in the process of heading toward the deeper water, when the Navy approached. Afraid to get caught with incriminating evidence, they opened the seacocks and flooded the ship!"

"What happened to the crew?"

"They offloaded onto a high-powered skiff and raced toward the shore along the coast of Sorrento."

"No one caught them at Sorrento?"

Sam shook his head. "A car was waiting for them, and the crew split up…"

"Someone knew exactly what they were doing."

Sam sighed. "And we're going to find out who."

Sam and Tom worked quickly to set up their SCUBA equipment. Sam slid into his wetsuit. They were diving on trimix — a unique combination of oxygen, helium, and nitrogen designed to allow a diver to reach extraordinary depths.

The plan was to reach the bridge and remove the AIS hard drive. Failing that, if they could locate the ship's unique AIS code, they might be able to retrospectively locate where the ship had been over the months leading up to the loss of the Phoenix. Either way, they wouldn't know until they were inside the wreckage.

Tom glanced at the schematics. Speaking to Elise, he asked, "Are you sure the hard drive's going to work after being submerged in saltwater?"

"Certain. Cyber criminals have been trying to work out how to permanently destroy data from hard drives since the first personal computer was invented. It's much harder said than done."

"Really? I didn't know."

Elise nodded. "Saltwater, fire, smashing with hammers… generally result in them still being able to be retrieved by technicians with enough know-how."

Sam raised his eyebrows. "So what do we need when we want to wipe a hard drive?"

"A magnet."

"Really?"

"Yeah. It wipes everything from the hard drive, rendering any data useless."

Sam said, "That's fascinating. I'll keep it in mind next time I want to erase my hard drive."

Tom shrugged. "Hey, I'm good to go."

"All right, all right." Sam picked up his full faced dive mask with a built in push to talk radio transmitter. "We'll see you in an hour, Elise."

Enjoy," she replied with her eyes still fixated on her laptop screen. "I'll see if I can find the aircraft that flew using the Phoenix Flight 318's transponder code."

"Good luck."

Sam stepped off the aft deck of the *Moonlight Sonata* into the warm waters of the Tyrrhenian Sea. He and Tom quickly checked their gauges and dive computers.

Everything was in order.

Sam turned to Tom, and asked, "You good to dive?"

"All good buddy, let's go see what the *San Juan* is hiding from the world."

They made the descent quickly.

It was good to be diving in warm water for a change.

The wreck of the *San Juan* came into view. It listed entirely on its starboard side. Large swathes of floating cardboard sheeting surrounded the wreck, showing clearly how the cargo ship had managed to stay hidden for so long—someone had been creatively altering the topside shape to confuse anyone searching with satellite images.

The bridge was one of those aft towers that rose multiple stories above the main deck. It had a narrow open deck running on the outside of the bridge to the port and starboard side, like a slim wing. The starboard side was buried deep in the sandy seabed, but the opening was clearly accessible on the portside.

Sam pointed to the opening and he and Tom swam toward it. The hatch was a heavy steel watertight door with a thick latch on the inside and outside that allowed it to be battened down in a severe storm.

He unlatched the door, and pulled on its handle.

The door swung open with ease and they both swam through.

Sam switched on his flashlight.

Although there was plenty of light descending through the clear water, it was much darker inside the bridge. Despite its odd angle, the bridge looked undamaged. It was typical for a cargo ship, with a large fishbowl shaped windshield above an array of mechanical controls, instruments and navigation charts.

Sam ran the beam of his flashlight across the bridge, from port to starboard. The digitally fortified bridge was a far cry from the command centers of bygone merchant ships. Instruments ran the entire length of the bridge, with the helm placed at the center, in a position of command.

Along the portside instrument panel stood the navigation station with GPS, digital maps, and Admiralty charts, to the right of which, stood a large monitor with the Electronic Chart Display and Information System (ECDIS), a geographic information system used for nautical navigation. Beneath the ECDIS system was a steel cupboard that housed a series of fiber optic cables which ran underneath the workstation into two motherboards. Attached were two small digital boxes — presumably hard drives — which appeared somewhat unimpressive compared to the size of the ship.

Tom shined his flashlight right on it.

A yellow imprint read, *Backup AIS hard drive.*

Sam pulled it free from the fiber optic cable that connected it to the motherboard. The hard drive fit comfortably in the palm of his hand. He slipped it into the pocket of his buoyancy control device and zipped it up.

"That was quick," Tom said.

"And surprisingly easy," Sam replied. "It figures. The first time in months we've had the chance to dive in warm, equatorial waters."

Sam pushed himself back from the computer hub.

Facing forward, he spotted the lopsided view from the captain's chair. It showed three radar screens next to the helm.

Directly in front of him, above where his eyes would be if the ship was righted, were the ship's primary indicators, which had once showed the ship's course over ground, compass, depth, engine RPM, rate of turn, clock, and barometry.

Tom said, "What a waste. A perfectly good ship given a watery grave to cover something up."

Sam smiled. "Depending on what Elise finds on this hard drive, we might still have to find a way to bring the *San Juan* to the surface."

Beneath his dive mask Tom raised an incredulous eyebrow. "The bulk of the ship is sub-one hundred feet. It would be a nightmare to bring her to the surface."

"More importantly, it would take too long. We need answers now. But I don't see any other leads to go off if the hard drive's empty. Someone on board this vessel gave the perpetrators away, otherwise they would have never sunk it."

Tom nodded. "All right, let's head to the surface... see what we can find."

Sam turned toward the exit, switched his flashlight off, and said, "Stop."

Because, descending toward the door were two bright lights approaching like the eyes of a predator.

CHAPTER TWENTY-SEVEN

S AM RAN HIS EYES ACROSS the SCUBA divers.

Taking them in at a glance, he knew they weren't there for a recreational wreck dive. They carried Soviet era, Special Underwater Assault Rifle, called an APS. The weapons were AK-47 sized with a similar format, and sported a massive banana style magazine that contained some 26 self-contained rocket-like 5.66mm X 120mm dart cartridges. The APS was capable of unleashing its full dart barrage in a matter of seconds.

Tom said, "Down the stairs!"

"I'm on it!"

Sam kicked his fins hard, swimming down the internal stairwell. They had no way to tell if they had been seen or not. It didn't take long before their visibility in the dark reached zero and they were forced to switch their flashlights back on.

At the bottom of the bridge tower, Sam and Tom raced through the hull, searching for an exit point. With the ship listing over on its starboard side, most of the exterior portholes close to them were blocked. They swam quickly through the empty hull, popping up through a manhole nearly two hundred feet along the forward deck.

Sam switched off his flashlight. "Now what do you want to do?"

"We can't surface right now," Tom said. "They'd come straight after us."

"I have an idea."

Sam dived to the portside of the hull so that their attackers inside the bridge couldn't spot them. He then slipped behind the steel door which opened to the bridge. It was the only entry-exit point on that side of the ship.

Next to the door was an iron rod that could be used to batten down the door in case of a storm. It was designed to be used on the inside, but also fit the lock on the outside. Sam shoved it between the handle and the edge of the door, effectively jamming it shut.

The divers spotted him as he kicked his fins and started to swim toward the surface. They raced toward the now locked steel door, trying to kick their way out. It was a fruitless exercise. The door was designed to survive the wrath of the ocean during a violent storm.

Sam and Tom rapidly sped toward the surface, as the divers quickly disappeared into the internal bowels of the ship to find their own way out. It would take the divers some time to escape.

Sam exhaled as he and Tom made their ascent.

On the surface, they quickly climbed aboard the *Moonlight Sonata*, with Veyron and Matthew helping to pull their equipment in.

As soon as they were on board, Sam said, "Pauline, we've got company down below — get us out of here!"

Pauline didn't need to be told twice. She pushed the twin throttles all the way forward and the large pleasure cruiser took off like a racehorse.

Sam dried himself and stepped into the main living quarters, where Elise was still working on her laptop.

He placed the *San Juan's* AIS hard drive on the table next to her. "I got you a present."

She took it, smiled, and said, "That's great. I found you something while you were away, too."

"What?"

"An F16 Falcon Fighter."

Sam wiped his face with a towel. "Come again?"

"It was a US F16 Falcon Fighter which took off on the same morning the Phoenix Flight 318 went missing. It flew across Portugal and above the Mediterranean Sea before looping back around and landing on board the US aircraft carrier, the *CVS Harry S Truman*."

"Are you sure?"

Elise pointed to a series of photos on her laptop. "The times match up exactly."

Sam ran the palms of his hands across his forehead and through his hair. "You've got to be kidding me."

Tom stepped into the room, having heard the last comment. "You think the US government was responsible?"

Elise said, "I'm almost certain of it. The satellite surveillance system was intentionally switched off during a fifteen-minute window when the fighter jet crossed Portugal. This means someone from inside the US Defense Department made the conscious decision to hide these events."

Tom said, "The question is why?"

"There's only one answer I can think of…" Sam said, through gritted teeth. "The US Defense Department authorized the sanction of Phoenix Airlines flight 318!"

CHAPTER TWENTY-EIGHT

Pentagon

S AM REILLY ENTERED THE OFFICE of the Secretary of Defense.

It was a large room with blue carpet, a massive desk, and two small tables for meetings—four seats each. It wasn't the kind of place for a big, open meeting. Just a few generals and maybe a head of state or two. Secrets passed through the innocuous room day and night. The carpet was new, and the rich mahogany door had been replaced since the last time he was here.

He closed his mind to the recent memory.

The last time he'd been in the room, he'd been kidnapped. The event had very nearly cost him his life, while proving that no matter how much of a mutually beneficial relationship he shared with the Secretary of Defense, he would always be just a pawn in the large machine of justice, and as such, the US Defense could readily sacrifice him at a whim or out of necessity.

Either way, he didn't want to be that pawn.

"Sit," the Secretary of Defense commanded without meeting his eye.

"Yes, ma'am."

He took a seat on one of the leather couches, leaned back, and folded his hands across his lap. A new painting of the President hung where his abductor had shot a warning shot the last time he was there.

The door was closed by an aide.

The inconspicuous air-tight seal made Sam's ears pop.

They were now alone.

The Secretary of Defense finished reading whatever it was that she was working on in silence. Sam waited with practiced patience.

She stood up and greeted him with a firm handshake. She was a slim but muscular woman with stark red hair. Intelligent, commanding, and always intimidating, she wore her dark business suit and her permanent scowl with equal severity.

Her face softened. "How are you feeling, Sam?"

"Fine."

"I mean after your ordeal."

Sam's jaw clenched for a second. "I knew you were talking about my abduction. Bad things happen. I came out all right."

"Good." The Secretary of Defense didn't achieve her position by spending a lot of time discussing other people's feelings. Without further preamble, she said, "You wanted to talk to me about a delicate matter?"

"Yes." Sam set his jaw and looked directly at her, and said, "I want to know what our involvement was in the loss of Phoenix Airlines flight 318?"

Her trimmed eyebrow arched. "Our involvement?"

Sam quickly brought her up to speed with what they knew about the bogus A380 at the bottom of Calypso Deep, the search and discovery of the *San Juan,* and the strange correlation of an F16 Falcon Fighter that carried the Phoenix's identical transponder codes.

She opened her mouth to protest that the US government does not sanction the abduction of commercial jets carrying hundreds of people. Then she met his steely blue eyes and penetrating gaze and it changed her mind. "I'll make some delicate inquiries."

"Thank you, ma'am."

Her emerald green eyes locked on his. "Anything else, Mr. Reilly?"

"No, ma'am."

"Good day then."

Sam stood up and walked out of her office. He followed the hallway that ran from the northern wedge to the outer rim of the Pentagon.

On his way out, he nodded to the Chairman of the Joint Chiefs of Staff, General Painter, and the Director of the CIA, Ross Jarratt. Both men made the slightest of nods in recognition, without slowing their stride.

Outside the Pentagon, Sam's cell phone started to ring.

He answered it on the first ring. Caller ID informed him it was Elise. He said, "Could you extract the AIS data from the *San Juan's* hard drive?"

"Yes."

"What did you find?"

"Two months before the Phoenix disappeared, the *San Juan* was on a routine run through Panama to Europe. They made a course deviation of three degrees, amounting to a total of ten miles worth of detour to stop at a small island in the Caribbean. It stayed there for twenty-four hours before continuing on to Athens."

"Why?"

"According to their records, the unplanned stop had to do with engine problems, but it never identified what or how the problem was rectified. It was there less than twenty-four hours, before it got underway again."

Sam crunched his face up tight. "What do satellite images of the island show?"

"Not much. The island looks like a pretty desolate wasteland, a rocky outcrop, nothing more. It was impossible to camouflage an A380, let alone land one. No hangers. Nowhere to hide."

"Interesting."

"There's something else, too."

Sam unlocked his car and got in. "What?"

"We checked with local air traffic controllers…"

"And?"

"One of them gave an incredible story about a mayday he heard three days after the Phoenix Flight 318 had disappeared. He said that a man named Andrew Goddard had woken up to an entire cabin full of unconscious passengers and crew. He was requesting help to land the damned thing."

"A ghost plane," Sam said, his voice severe. "It's Helios Flight 522 all over again!"

On August 14, 2005, the pilots of a passenger jet travelling between Cyprus and Athens stopped responding to air traffic control. When fighter jets were scrambled, they found a chilling sight. The aircraft was on autopilot, but the pilots, as well as the passengers and crew, were all slumped forward, unconscious. It turned out to be a problem with pressurization, causing everyone on board to pass out.

To add to the mystery of the tragedy, fighter pilots noticed a flight attendant enter the cockpit at the last minute, carrying an oxygen bottle. The flight attendant's name was later discovered to be Andreas Prodromou. He entered the cockpit and sat down in the captain's seat, having remained conscious by using a portable oxygen supply. Prodromou held a UK Commercial

Pilot License, but was not qualified to fly the Boeing 737. Prodromou waved at the F16s very briefly, but almost as soon as he entered the cockpit, the left engine flamed out due to fuel exhaustion, followed by the right ten minutes later, causing the aircraft to crash into hills near Grammatiko, killing all 121 passengers and crew on board.

It was a chilling thought. Elise expelled her breath. "Right... only this time, the aircraft didn't crash."

Sam asked, "So why didn't the air traffic controller report it?"

"He said that he thought it was a hoax at the time. Still does. Didn't want to stir up false hope with the grieving families."

Sam squinted his eyes in the bright sun. "How close to the island did the radio transmission originate from?"

Elise said, "A hundred and five miles out."

"Good God, that's the place."

"Looks like it," Elise replied. "I've organized to charter a local trawling vessel... and I've booked you on a flight to Puerto Rico."

CHAPTER TWENTY-NINE

Office of the Chairman of the Joint Chiefs of Staff, Pentagon

GENERAL PAINTER, THE CHAIRMAN OF the Joint Chiefs of Staff watched Sam Reilly's car drive off from his window. His face was set hard. He breathed heavily and he found his stomach churning with fear.

He slammed the surveillance file down on his desk. "Ah, hell. How did he get involved in this?"

"I don't know, sir," Ross Jarratt, the Director of the CIA replied.

General Painter was fuming. "How the hell did Phoenix 318 get so close to Grenada?"

"We don't know, sir."

"Don't give me that shit. The aircraft landed, so our people must know what happened."

"It's a wet operation." Jarratt locked eyes with the General in defiance. "For reasons of accountability and deniability, you weren't supposed to know."

"Yeah, well neither was the rest of the world, but all that's about to be blown out into the open. So you'd better tell me what the fuck went wrong!"

Jarratt waved his hand placatingly. "All right, all right. There was a passenger. Someone on board woke up first. Maybe a couple minutes before our agents. Maybe ten minutes. We don't know how long for sure. Either way, he managed to reach the cockpit."

"Good God! How did you let this happen?"

"Our team got control of the situation in time."

General Painter boomed, "Obviously they didn't if Sam Reilly is hearing about it from an Air Traffic Controller from fucking Grenada! How long do you think it's going to take him to make the damned connection?"

Ross Jarratt made a dramatic sigh. "What do you want me to do?"

"Nothing. Sam Reilly's the Secretary of Defense's pet. She'll move Heaven and Earth to get to the bottom of it if he goes missing."

"We can't let him find the truth," Jarratt said heavily. "The entire world would be up in arms if they knew what we've done."

"Agreed."

"So what the hell are we going to do?"

"Shut him down. Every step of the way. Block him."

Jarratt said, "He won't like that."

Painter slammed his fist on the table. "I don't care what he damn well likes!"

"What if he puts up a fight?"

General painter slid the Director of the CIA a piece of paper.

Jarratt read it and then swallowed hard. "Is the President aware of this, sir?"

"He signed it, didn't he?"

Jarratt's eyes returned to the bottom of the page. "You're right." Then he read the order out loud. "Having exhausted all other efforts to silence him with regard to Phoenix Flight 318, you're authorized to kill Sam Reilly."

"I'm not proud of it, but there's nothing we can do. The man can't be bought, he won't listen to reason, he has a distorted view of honor and patriotism—if he gets in our way, we're just going to have to kill him." The General crossed his arms. "Who do you have running the operation?"

"Rhyse Vaughn."

"Really?"

Jarratt raised his eyebrow. "You don't like him?"

General Painter shook his head. "The man's a pompous ass!"

Jarratt made a half-shrug with his shoulders. "The man attended Exeter as a boy, then Yale as a man, before the CIA picked him up because of his unique and rather delicate psychometric scores, which identified him for our very specific line of work. His father was a senator, his mother a model, and his grandfather an oil tycoon, so I really can't see that he had any other choice than to become what he is. Besides, as it turns out, he's the best operative the CIA's ever had."

Painter nodded. "But can you control him?"

"I'll admit that's difficult, but we don't have to. He believes in the cause as much as we do. He'll kill to keep the secret."

Painter swallowed. "I'm not worried about that. My only concern is if he can be trained to stop killing once this thing is over."

Ross Jarratt nodded hesitantly, and bit his lower lip. He breathed out. "That, I don't know."

CHAPTER THIRTY

Puerto Rico, Caribbean Sea

T HE CARIBBEAN SEA WAS HOME to twenty-eight island nations and more than seven thousand individual islands.

Sam Reilly wore an overtly touristy Hawaiian shirt, board shorts, and sandals as he made his way from the Luis Muñoz Marín international airport to the Hilton, where he'd booked a suite for the week. He thanked his taxi driver, checked in, and advised hotel staff that he wished to be left alone for the extent of his stay. Truth be told, he had no intention of staying in the hotel at all. But given his own government's potential involvement, he wanted them to believe he'd finally taken that much anticipated vacation. After throwing his bag of limited luggage next to the bed, he made his way down the beach.

The white sand mingled with the shallow waves of the Caribbean to form a soft bay, filled with hues of soft blues and emerald green water. Not more than a hundred feet out were some thirty luxury yachts, pleasure cruisers, and a single seaplane. These were toys for the wealthy tourists who had come to enjoy the pristine waters. Just out from those, were a myriad of older vessels, tenderly identified as rust buckets.

Hidden among these was the *Alessandra*, a retired fishing trawler, turned Caribbean houseboat for two self-professed and permanent vagabonds. Sam's sharp eyes locked onto the old vessel. Only two people were visible on its deck. He recognized both of them from the text Elise had sent, but otherwise had never seen either of them before.

Sam placed his shirt and sandals at the edge of the beach, above the high-water mark, and stepped down to the water. He entered the water, wading until the gentle waves lapped at his waist, and then dived into the water.

He swam purposefully toward the expensive pleasure cruisers first, ogling them like a tourist dreaming about another life. By the time he'd drifted sufficiently far enough from the beach to avoid prying eyes, he casually swam toward the *Alessandra*. At the surface, twenty or so feet from the rusty old fishing trawler, he dived under the water, beneath the boat's keel, and surfaced on the side opposite the Puerto Rican beach.

A rope ladder hung unceremoniously from the starboard taffrail. Sam gripped the ladder and pulled himself up, sliding over the rail and quickly taking cover in the enclosed pilothouse.

"Welcome aboard, Sam," Tom Bower greeted him with a warm smile. "I should have been expecting pirates given the sea we're traveling."

Sam shook his hand. "Thank you. Have you got the equipment on board?"

"Everything you asked for."

Tom rapped his knuckles on top of the pilot house. A moment later Sam heard the big diesel engine turn over, followed by the run of the anchor chain being drawn into its locker. The heavy driveshaft made a loud crank sound, as it was shifted into forward gear. Sam braced onto the side of the hull, as the *Alessandra* began motoring to the southeast.

About ten minutes later, once they were out of sight from the Puerto Rican coastline, Sam and Tom stepped out onto the deck. A tan woman in her mid-forties stood at the helm, while a man of fifty worked around the forward deck, clearing rope lines, and preparing the vessel for their crossing before approaching them.

Tom said, "Sam, may I introduce the owners of the *Alessandra*, Amy and Colin Moriarty."

Sam met their eyes, "Pleased to meet you both."

"The pleasure's mine," Colin replied, his voice a deep baritone, his accent clearly British. He offered his hand. "I read about your discovery of the Mahogany Ship in Australia a few years ago. It was a fascinating read. Made me wonder how much of it was made up and how much of it was mere legend."

Sam took his hand, feeling the firm and leathery grip of the seasoned sailor. He opened his mouth to speak, made a half-grin, and then said, "I've often said that some of the best legends are buried in hidden truths."

Amy made a wry smile, her hazel eyes which matched her olive skin, held his gaze with piercing scrutiny. "So was the Mahogany Ship based more on truth or lies?"

She spoke with a crisp Londoner accent, fulfilling Sam's impression that they were both British expats.

Sam said, "To be honest, it was based on a whole bunch of both."

She arched an eyebrow. "Really?"

Sam nodded. "Yeah. The ship existed. The legend was true and its old owners controlled unimaginable powers. Like anything capable of supplying great power, lies and deceit followed like hungry jackals, leading to the death of all who trailed in its wake."

She laughed at that. "How did you get out alive?"

"That's easy."

Colin's eyes narrowed. "This I've got to hear."

Sam said, "I didn't try to covet its power. Instead I sought only the truth."

Everyone remained silent for a few seconds.

And then they all started laughing.

Colin placed his hand on Sam's shoulder and gripped it gently. "You're really something, Sam Reilly!"

"You look tired," Amy said, meeting Sam's eye. "Do you want Tom to show you the bunking arrangements?"

"Yes please," Sam replied. "I haven't slept since I left Italy, more than twenty-four hours ago."

"Well, enjoy your sleep. It's nearly twenty-four hours before we reach the island."

"Thank you," Sam said. "Both of you. We really appreciate your help."

Colin shook his head. "Don't thank us too much. Tom's paid us the price we requested in US dollars. It's enough to pay for our meager expenses over the next year—and like I told the woman on the phone—I think she said her name was Elise?— we're not going anywhere near the island. We're just going to be dropping you nearby. For the last bit, you're on your own. Tom, you said you've got that covered, didn't you?"

Tom nodded. "Yeah, I've brought two sea scooters—fully charged with a range of ten miles."

Sam glanced at Amy and Colin. "All the same, I appreciate your help."

"You're welcome," they both replied.

Tom led Sam down into the main hold, past a large private cabin to the forward storage locker which had been converted into a makeshift berth, where two hammocks hung from beams above like a 17th century Spanish Galleon.

Sam ran his eyes across the sleeping arrangements and back to Tom. "Nice accommodation you organized for us."

"I thought you would approve."

Sam clambered onto the hammock, nearly falling out the first time he tried. On the second attempt he managed the task with more than a little bit of athleticism.

Tom said, "What do you think?"

"It's comfortable. Good night."

"No," Tom said. "I meant about the plan."

"It's good," Sam said. "We'll find out if the island's concealing the passengers and crew of Phoenix Flight 318 tomorrow. After that, we can deal with it one way or the other."

"All right. Good night." Tom went to leave and stopped. "Was there anything else? You look worried?"

"No, I'm all right. Just sleep deprived." Sam's eyebrows furrowed. "There is one thing that keeps bugging me."

"What?"

Sam grinned. "In Sherlock Holmes, was Moriarty the villain or the hero?"

CHAPTER THIRTY-ONE

T HE *ALESSANDRA* MOTORED ON THROUGH the day and into the night.

Sam opened his eyes. It was dark and he couldn't see much. The temperature had dropped to a more bearable 80 degrees Fahrenheit. His tongue felt dry. The air was humid and stale. He fumbled out of the hammock and climbed the stairs into the pilothouse.

On the deck Colin was barbequing a locally caught fish below a sky blazing with stars. Though Sam had no idea what type of fish it was, its smell wafted pleasingly and he breathed deeply. A timid breeze blew from the south, bringing with it cooler air.

Colin asked, "How did you sleep?"

"Good." His eyes ran across the calm waters through to the horizon. They were in the open waters of the Caribbean Sea, but at a glance they might as well have been in the Pacific or Atlantic Ocean. There wasn't even the sight of another vessel in the distance. "Where are we?"

"About a hundred miles out from Grenada." Colin glanced at the digital map beside the helm and squinted. "About a hundred and forty from the island."

"Right," Sam said, taking that in. "Has it ever had a name?"

Amy stepped up from the galley carrying a bottle of red wine. "Anyone want a drink?"

Colin said, "Yes please, beautiful."

"No thanks," Sam said.

Colin took a drink from his glass. "Sorry, what were you asking, Sam?"

"Did the island ever have a name?"

"What?" Colin spread his hands, holding the barbeque tongs out like a question mark. "The island?"

"Yeah."

"No. It was originally part of the Grenada owned islands, known as the Spice Isles. But somewhere in the last fifty years, the Grenadian government abdicated ownership."

Sam raised his eyebrows. "Why?"

"No one knows."

"You mean they simply abandoned it?"

"No. They definitely abdicated ownership." Colin expelled a deep breath. "They even made a big show of saying that they no longer owned the island."

"So someone bought it?"

"Who knows? Maybe. All I know is that the locals call it the ghost island because no one goes in and no one ever comes out."

Sam arched his eyebrow with incredulity. "A ghost island?"

"Look... I know what you're thinking, but the locals and everyone who's spent any time sailing in these waters, will tell you that strange things happen on that island. No one has been there in the past ten years since we've been cruising in these parts — but that doesn't stop the strange comings and goings."

"Strange comings and goings?"

"Weird noises," Colin said, keeping his palms turned

skyward, like he already knew how crazy that must sound. "Shrieks that reach out across the bay."

Amy put in, "Kind of like a howling sound."

Sam said, "No boats ever go there?"

"No. Never."

"What about aircraft?"

"No never," Colin was emphatic.

Amy tilted her head, turning her eyes away from his gaze. "Except…"

Sam's eyes narrowed. "What is it?"

Colin's tone was defiant. "It's nothing."

Sam nodded. "That might be the case, but it might still be useful to our investigation."

"I don't intend to get dragged into court over this."

"You won't. No one will ever hear about your involvement on the island. I promise."

Amy said, "It's all right, Colin. We're already involved just by offering them passage. No reason we might not tell them the truth."

Sam met her eye. "What's the truth?"

"People have seen some other strange things radiating from the island."

"Like what?"

"There's a powerful light, it's purple and shoots up toward the sky — nearly a thousand feet at least — lighting up the entire island."

Sam grinned. "You're kidding me?"

"No. I'm serious. We've even seen it a couple times ourselves."

Sam mulled that over for a moment, trying to find a reasonable explanation. Unable to find one, he asked, "What's stopping people from visiting the island?"

"What do you mean?" Colin asked. "I told you, no one goes in and no one goes out."

"Sure. But why?"

Colin's response was curt. "Because they don't!"

"Sure, but someone must have tried once or twice. I mean, what about someone who's not local. A vagabond like yourselves, who's just crossed the Atlantic, and feels like heaving to under the lee of the island? Maybe someone like that has gone in and explored the island."

"Not that we've heard of," Amy said. "Instead, what we've heard is that a couple times a year empty boats drift out to sea from the island. Some of them are recognized by local sailors, others look like they're sailing yachts that have come—like you suggested before, from across the Atlantic—but all of them share one similarity."

"What's that?"

"They're all riddled with bullet holes. Some have blood inside. Never bodies—living or dead. Just a lot of blood."

"Interesting," Sam said. Turning to Colin he asked, "Before you sounded like you had an explanation, but weren't sure if you wanted to voice it. Care to share?"

The muscles around Colin's jaw tightened. "I'd rather not."

"What if it might save Tom and my life?" Sam held his breath. "They say knowledge is power. Right now, all we know is that we're going into a ghost island that keeps sending bullet ridden boats back out to sea. Care to shed any more light on what you suspect is going on out there on the island?"

Colin opened his mouth to speak and closed it again. He took a deep breath. "All right. But you're not going to like it."

Sam said, "Go on."

"It's an old US military base."

"Really? There's no record of the US government ever owning it."

"There wouldn't be, would there?"

"Why?"

"Because they're doing illegal experiments on people."

CHAPTER THIRTY-TWO

A T EIGHT-THIRTY A.M. THE *Alessandra* dropped anchor roughly three miles out from the island, putting up a set of offshore fishing rods just for good measure.

Sam examined the shoreline with a pair of high-powered binoculars.

His brow furrowed.

Tom asked, "What's wrong?"

Sam handed him the binoculars. "Here, have a look for yourself."

Tom took them, adjusting the lens into focus. "I thought the place was meant to be a barren wasteland filled with volcanic rock?"

"Yeah, me too."

Instead, it was covered with the dense vegetation of a tropical jungle. At a glance, it was easy to imagine someone hiding anything from the remains of an A380 through to a government's illegal laboratory, where they tested human subjects.

Sam stepped down into the pilothouse and opened his

laptop. He brought up the most recent satellite image, taken about an hour earlier, and then emailed by Elise.

He studied the images. Where the island was covered in dense jungle now appeared to be volcanic rock, the island looked barren in the satellite photographs.

Tom stared at the laptop from over Sam's shoulder. "Well, that's strange."

Sam made a spooky sound with his voice. "See, that's why they call it a strange island."

"Somehow I'm not buying it."

Sam met his eye. "You think it's all a giant trick done by mirrors? Some sort of sleight of hand done on a large scale?"

"Yep. Beats me how they're doing it. But they've already proven they're not lacking in technical resources."

"I wonder if Elise has any ideas. More importantly, I wonder if she could get us an image of the island that looks more like it does in real life."

"Try her."

Sam picked up the satellite phone and dialed Elise's number from memory.

"How's Puerto Rico?" she asked.

"Nice. I'll let you know when we get back there."

"What can I do for you, Sam?"

"The images you sent of the island this morning… where did they come from?"

"It's a satellite surveillance system, originally built for the Pentagon, but now used by a number of agencies, ranging from the Department of Defense, through to Search and Rescue. The images were taken at 07:04 today, so they should be the most up to date. Why?"

"They're fakes."

"What do you mean, fakes?"

"They show a desolate island without any vegetation."

"And?"

"I'm looking at the island through binoculars and the entire thing is as thick as the Colombian jungle."

There was silence on the line for a few seconds.

"Did you hear what I said, Elise?"

"I heard you, Sam. That's really interesting."

"You have a theory?"

"Sure, I do."

Sam grinned. "You want to share that theory?"

"It has nothing to do with the island...."

"Then why can't we get a good visual?"

"I don't think it has anything to do with the island..."

"Meaning?"

"I believe someone from the CIA has intentionally altered the satellite surveillance system to make it appear different."

CHAPTER THIRTY-THREE

SAM AND TOM DROPPED OVER the *Alessandra's* rail simultaneously.

Sam waited a moment until he was just a few feet underwater, and pressed the start button on his RS1 Military Grade Sea Scooter. Nearby, Tom did the same. The underwater diver propulsion vehicles were small, hand-held, electric devices used by SCUBA divers and free-divers for underwater propulsion. They weighed less than twenty pounds each, and had a water bladder, designed to automatically control the diver's buoyancy.

"Are you ready?" Sam asked, speaking into the underwater radio mounted into his full face mask.

"Good to go," Tom replied.

"All right, let's go kick over a hornet's nest."

He used his right thumb to depress the speed rate button, and the little propeller began to spin with a whine. The RS1 Sea Scooter had three speed settings. Sam checked his compass bearing, and then flicked the setting to its fastest speed.

The sea scooter raced forward toward the island,

maneuvering like a small motorcycle underwater. It was nearly four miles to their south, which took them forty-two minutes to reach. They slowed their speed as they brought the sea scooters into a fringing coral reef through a narrow channel. The satin water turned into a vibrant landscape of colorful fish on a canvas of blue, green, and yellow coral that climbed out from a bed of seaweed, filled with brown and orange hues.

Sam eased his sea scooter toward the shore. Several banded sea snakes, with their classic white and black stripes, swam by with indifference. Sam and Tom shuffled out of their way. The highly venomous snakes rarely attacked humans, but no reason to tempt fate.

Above a small crevasse in the coral reef, Sam cut the power to his sea scooter, and flooded its buoyancy control bladder, making it sink to the bottom. Tom copied him, bringing his scooter around and laying it down side by side in the shallow reef. Both then removed their scuba gear, grabbed their waterproof carry bags, and swam to the surface — leaving all of their dive equipment carefully hidden beneath the reef.

With just his dive mask on, Sam swam to the shore.

On the beach, the two men quickly made their way into the shelter of the thick tropical jungle. Concealed by the vegetation, Sam opened his water tight bag. Inside he removed a towel and dried himself, before putting on another Hawaiian shirt — there must have been a special on at the local giftshop. He then laid the towel on the ground and then, almost ritualistically, he placed his Heckler and Koch MP5 on it.

The nine-millimeter, German designed, submachine gun was popular with military divers around the world, because its sealed chamber gave it excellent reliability even fully submerged. He removed the magazine, opened the chamber and checked that it was free from any bullets. It was clean and its parts were well oiled. He then tested the firing mechanism. It tapped forward with a firm clicking sound.

He grinned. "All right. Let's go."

Tom secured his submachinegun and nodded. "Let's go see what secrets this ghost island wants to release."

They hugged the jungle, following the beach until they reached a well worn path leading to the center of the small island.

Above the chirp of tropical birds, came another sound resonating from the middle of the island's hidden interior.

Sam paused, cocking his ears to listen. "What is that sound?"

Tom bit his lower lip. "I don't know. It's not natural, that much I know for sure."

"Yeah, but what could it be?"

"I don't know."

They continued nearly half a mile before the sound became loud enough for them to make out its origins.

Sam swept the dense jungle, trying to locate the sound's origins. "Do you hear that?"

"Sure, but I don't believe it."

"No. So much for a ghost island."

"Indeed..." Tom raised his eyebrows. "Unless, that's the sound of ghost-laughing."

Sam grinned slightly. "Come on, let's go find out."

The trail rose to a narrow crest. They both ducked down, edging their way to the top on their bellies to get a better view.

Looking down on the opening far below, Sam shook his head in disbelief. Hundreds of people were playing on a sandy clearing—say, four or five hundred to be exact—the same amount one would expect to be onboard an A380 superjumbo. They were all dressed in an array of beach attire, well suited to their deserted island retreat. The men wore board shorts and for those who wore any shirts at all, they appeared floral and had a Hawaiian theme. The women were in a combination of bikinis, board shorts, or a mixture of the two.

The tourists were spread out, enjoying an array of different pleasure activities you'd expect at any resort island. Some played beach volleyball in the sand, others played tennis on a pair of tennis courts, while others simply sunbaked, basking in the warmth of the Caribbean sun. To the north, more than thirty people were drinking cocktails beside a crystal-clear spring.

Tom's lips curled upward into a wry grin. "Well, Sam... I have to admit, that's a sight I was not ready for."

"I agree. What sort of prison is this?"

"Beats me."

Sam grinned. "Let's go find out."

CHAPTER THIRTY-FOUR

TOM SAID, "AT LEAST WE'RE well dressed for the occasion."

"You're right," Sam agreed, trying to conceal his MP5 submachinegun beneath his Hawaiian shirt.

They followed the trail until they got closer, before diverting into the jungle to avoid being seen and skirting the clearing.

On the opposite side of the island, they came out of the jungle on a tropical paradise. There were a group of people in their twenties playing beach volleyball in board shorts and bikinis. A couple older people were snorkeling in the turquoise water. The thick canopy of the jungle extended right to the beach, which was no more than a few yards to the water.

"Some paradise these drug dealers have here for themselves," Sam said.

Tom shrugged. "Hey, crime pays until you get caught."

"Sure, but caught doing what, exactly?"

"I have no idea. This has got to be where someone's keeping the passengers and crew of the Phoenix, but for what purpose I can't even imagine."

"Ransom?"

"It's been more than three months. Who ever heard of someone keeping this number of prisoners happy for three months without making any ransom demands?"

"Beats me." Sam turned to keep heading around the island. "Let's keep going around the island. We need some definitive proof if we're to organize a rescue operation."

Tom asked, "Like what?"

Sam crossed his arms. "The A380 would be nice. A runway long enough for it to land would also help."

"Okay, let's keep going."

Behind them, a woman said, "Hey, you two weren't on the flight!"

"And what flight would that be?" Sam asked.

The woman swallowed hard, her eyes widening with fear. "I'm sorry it doesn't matter. The point is, you don't belong here, do you?"

Tom asked, "How would you know that? Maybe we paid for a lovely vacation on this beautiful island, like everyone else?"

The woman was about to argue against that point, but stopped short when she spotted someone approach.

"You're not supposed to be here!" A young woman, no more than eighteen approached wearing a blue, striped bikini. Beneath her smoking hot body, Sam noticed fine definition in her muscles, as though her figure was the product of hard work, not for show, rather than the other way round.

Sam met her eye, holding her gaze, without any more than a glance at the way her perfect, supple body was encased in the bikini. "Why not?"

"It's going to make them very angry. You should leave!"

"Make who angry?" Sam stopped. "Where exactly are we?"

The woman set her jaw, her reply curt, removing her original appearance of a young socialite. "I don't know what you think you're doing here, but you're not helping anyone. You need to leave before you ruin everything!"

An older man came up from the beach. His face was surly and his tone violent. "Get out of here! What do you think you're doing? You have no idea how much harm you're going to do!"

The first woman approached slowly. "They're not going to be happy with us."

"Who's not going to be happy?" Sam asked, backing away. "Are you prisoners?"

The woman in the striped bikini, who appeared to be in charge, said, "You don't understand. You couldn't! But you're making it worse for everyone. You need to go before you're spotted by THEM!"

"Who are THEY?"

"We're not supposed to talk to strangers. THEY said you might come. This will all be over soon, but not if you interrupt it. THEY'LL do it again if they have to." The woman's voice was pleading. "Please, don't make them do it again."

Sam felt constricted by their advancements. None of them were armed, but they didn't need to be. Outnumbered by the mob of apparent tourists, they could easily become overwhelmed.

Tom said, "I think I've seen enough."

"Yep, me too," Sam said. "Time to go."

CHAPTER THIRTY-FIVE

SAM AND TOM RACED ALL the way back to the *Alessandra*.
They climbed the rope ladder, handing their sea scooters to Amy and Colin, who pulled them on board their houseboat.

Amy said, "Welcome back. So what did you find? Any ghosts on your island?"

Sam shook his head. "No ghost. Only some of the happiest prisoners of all time."

Colin tilted his head, meeting his eye. "They're holding people prisoner on the island?"

"It appears so."

"What are you going to do about it?" Colin asked.

"That's a good question," Sam replied, swallowing hard. "If you're right and this whole place is an offshore interrogation center to process people for the CIA, then we're not going to be very popular with our own government."

Amy said, "All the same, maybe it should be disclosed."

"Yeah, I've got some connections in the Department of Defense. I'll come up with something. This isn't just an

American thing. There were people from all around the world on board that flight."

Sam's satellite phone started to ring.

The number was a UK country code. It was Sandi Larson, the anthropologist he'd met in Colorado.

He squinted his eyes. "What did you find?"

"You're not going to believe this…"

"Try me…"

"I dated the mask using a type of uranium-thorium dating method. Unlike other commonly used radiometric dating techniques such as rubidium–strontium or uranium–lead dating, the uranium-thorium technique does not measure accumulation of a stable end-member decay product. Instead, it calculates an age from…"

Sam interrupted her, "I trust your methods, Sandi. What did you find?"

"I'm glad you have a high opinion of me. But all the same, I didn't trust their results. That's why I ran it by three leading physicists—experts in the field of uranium-thorium dating."

"And… what did they find?"

"I don't know what to tell you, Mr. Reilly… but the evidence is undisputed."

"Sandi… what did you find?"

"The mask we brought out of the Colorado mine shaft… it was forged one hundred and four thousand years ago."

"Say that again…"

"The mask was forged one hundred and four thousand years ago," Sandi said. "You know what makes that date so significant?"

Sam crunched the muscles in his face together. "I suppose that makes it by far the oldest known intricate relic made by man?"

"Sure… probably. But that's not what makes the date so

significant."

"What is it, then?"

"It also coincides with the last time Homo sapiens shared the Earth with six other subspecies of the genus, Homo — including Homo erectus, Homo floresiensis, Homo habilis, Homo heidelbergensis, Homo naledi, and Homo neanderthalensis."

Sam took a deep breath. "Sandi, what are you telling me?"

Sandi sighed heavily into the phone, leaving him in silence for a moment. "I don't have a clue what you're involved in. But whatever it is, it's been going on a long time. Much longer than the loss of Phoenix Flight 318."

CHAPTER THIRTY-SIX

Ghost Island, Caribbean Sea

T HE THREE SIKORSKY UH-60 BLACK Hawks took off from the deck of the UK Aircraft Carrier, the *HMS Ocean* as part of an international strike force that included US Navy SEALs, UK SAS, and an Italian Special Forces team from the 9th Parachute Assault Regiment.

In the back of the lead helicopter, Sam Reilly sat, trying to put together what had really happened on the island. After bringing the information to the US Secretary of Defense, who emphatically denied that America owned any small ghost island near Grenada on which to conduct illegal interrogations he suggested that maybe a multinational team including those nations most represented in the loss of the Phoenix, should storm the island. To his surprise, she agreed, putting the full force of the US Department of Defense behind the proposal.

The question remained, if the US government wasn't involved in the strange capture of the Phoenix, and the digital concealment of the island from satellite surveillance — who was?

The stealth helicopter, with its specialized materials and use of harsh angles and flat surfaces used to deflect radar, came in low across the surface of the stilled sea, banking as it reached the island, and flying over a clearing that ran half the length of the island in a north-south direction.

Flying in formation, the helicopters landed one by one in the middle of the clearing.

Sam stepped out, his boots sinking into the thick sandy ground below. He led the multinational strike force team to the accommodation buildings next to the tennis courts.

The smell of ammonia wafted through his nostrils.

It hadn't been there before. His mind considered what it might have been used for, and none of them were good.

The three separate teams of specialist forces infiltrated the forest, securing each place, section by section, until they reached the middle of the island.

Sam stared at the empty, sandy surface, where the tennis courts had been and swore—because all signs of the lost passengers and crew of Phoenix Flight 318 had disappeared.

The place was empty.

Everything had been destroyed.

The entire place reeked of ammonia.

Whatever had been going on there, someone went to great lengths to bury it.

CHAPTER THIRTY-SEVEN

S AM BOARDED THE HELICOPTER BACK to the *HMS Ocean*.
His satellite phone rang.

He answered it on the second ring.

It was Elise. Without preamble she said, "How did the operation go?"

"Badly. They cleared the island. There's nothing left but the overpowering smell of ammonia. The commander in charge of our operation blames Tom and me for the bad intel. I'm pretty certain the Phoenix was there, but it left without much of a trace."

"Really?"

Sam stared vacantly out the Sikorsky's window at the myriad of bright stars that filled the sky. "Yeah, it turns out they had covered the runway with sand to obscure it from someone taking high altitude aerial photographs. It wouldn't have been that hard to do. After all, they had about five hundred prisoners to help."

"I thought the reconnaissance photos showed the clearing to be too short for an A380 to ever land, let alone takeoff again?"

"They did."

"Yet, you're still certain you had the right place?"

"Yeah. It turned out that about half the trees were fake."

"Fake?" Her voice rose an audible octave. "This just gets better and better. Who goes to the trouble of moving what must have been tons upon tons of sand and migrating a set of artificial trees to produce a shroud of jungle?"

Sam made a half-shrug to himself. "I don't know. I suppose the same people who went to the trouble of sinking a steel and cardboard cutout of the aircraft to confuse investigators about the disappearance of the Phoenix."

"Touché."

"So, we're back to square one. Unless you happened to find a connection with the passenger... the one who made the mayday call, which local air traffic control authorities dismissed... what was his name?"

"Goddard. Andrew Goddard," Elise replied. "And, it just so happens, we might be in luck."

Sam said, "Go on."

"I have no idea how he ended up in the cockpit of that flight, or how he ended up losing his original battle for control of the aircraft, but I think I have an idea of why they wanted the Phoenix with him on board, to disappear."

"Why?"

"I've done some searching. Goddard was sixty-one years and forty-five days old when the Phoenix disappeared. He was born wealthy. An only child, he inherited his family's great fortune and a German title of baron. Despite this, he was a hard worker throughout his life, studying philosophy at the University of Heidelberg, before going on to do a PhD in fine arts and antiquities."

Sam asked, "What vocation did he end up following?"

"He became a rare antiquities dealer, specializing in ancient masks from around the world.

"And you want to know the kicker…"

"What?"

"He was on his way to Venice to look at the acquisition of an ancient stone mask—depicting what appears to be an early sculpture of *Homo floresiensis*."

Sam listened to the quiet whip of the stealth helicopter's rotor blades spinning above. His lips curled into a mask of wry incredulity. "You've got to be kidding me."

He knew the story of *Homo floresiensis* well. First discovered in the cave of Liang Bua on the tiny Indonesian island of Flores in 2003, archeologists still debated whether or not they were technically a previous subspecies of the genus *Homo*, or merely a mutation of *Homo erectus*, which had shrunk through the process of long-term isolation on the island and insular dwarfing. The island was known to have the remains of the extinct pygmy elephant Stegodon, which was also believed to have been caused by insular dwarfism.

Elise said, "I read the most recent archeology papers on the topic."

"And?"

"They became extinct somewhere in the vicinity of a hundred thousand years ago."

"That's quite a coincidence."

"That's what I was thinking." Elise said, "There's something else, too."

Sam felt his heart race. He was closing in on the truth. "What have you got?"

"A name and address of someone set to inherit from Andrew Goddard in the event he's declared *Death in Absentia*."

Sam closed his eyes, opened them again, glancing up at the stars above. "What difference does that make? Goddard needs to be dead for more than twelve months before *Death in Absentia* comes into effect."

"This guy wasn't a relative set to inherit his wealth."

"Who was he?"

"The name is Lorenzo De Luca. A permanent resident in Venice. By the looks of things, it would appear that the two men were part of some sort of secret society."

"For what?"

"It doesn't say. But, there's a covenant that's already come into effect that states in the event Goddard becomes incapacitated or unreachable, Lorenzo De Luca is to be guarded twenty-four hours a day at a secure location—a bodyguard detail paid for by a special trust."

"Why?"

"Because he's the only other person on Earth who knows where the *Neanderthal Mask* was being housed—and if something were to happen to him, they would risk the mask disappearing into oblivion for another millennia."

"Any idea where the man's hunkering down?"

"I'll text you the address."

"Thanks, Elise. Given what we know so far, I think it's safe to say that man's life is in danger."

CHAPTER THIRTY-EIGHT

Canal Grande, Venice

THE ANCIENT CITY OF VENICE spanned 117 small islands in the Venetian Lagoon, which connected to mainland Italy through the *Ponte della Libertia*.

Sam motored the old, wooden speed boat, into the Canal Grande — the largest canal which snaked through the medieval island, splitting it in two. He eased the throttle back, and the big V8 engine made a guttural roar, as though complaining about the restraint being enforced.

Next to him, Tom stared at the digital map.

Sam followed the inside channel as he meandered his way in from the south. His eyes met Tom's. "You know where we're going?"

"Not a clue. Everywhere looks the same to me."

Sam's cheeks dimpled with his big, toothy grin. "Thank the Gods for modern GPS, hey?"

"I'll say."

On their left they passed *Saint Mark's Basilica*, the island's largest patriarchal cathedral, with its massive domes dominating the ancient city's skyline in all their classic Italian-byzantine architecture. The motor made its constant thumping sound as its large V8 exhaust pipes begged to be released, and the propeller churned the water, creating a deep and turbid wake.

Up ahead, they reached the *Doge's Palace*.

Tom said, "Take the canal on the left."

Sam swung the wheel round to the left, and the motorboat obediently threaded its way into the small *Rio di Palazzo*, passing under the *Bridge of Sighs*. Sam glanced up at its distinctive white limestone, which formed the enclosed bridge that once connected the New Prison to the interrogation rooms in the *Doge's Palace*. Legend told that the bridge was named as such because it was the last view of Venice that a convict would see before their imprisonment.

They motored past the northern end of *Saint Mark's Basilica*, where hundreds of seagulls filled the *Piazza* and Tom said, "Take the right at the next church."

Sam's eyes narrowed. "Which church? We're in Italy — home of Catholicism. There's a church at the end of every street — or in this case, canal."

Tom smiled. "Just take the next right."

Sam pulled the motorboat to the far left, to make way for a small procession of oncoming gondolas. His eyes took in the rich landscape of Venetian architecture, before landing on a couple who seemed intent on getting the perfect kiss as their gondola made its way underneath one of the thousands of bridges that riddled the Venetian Lagoon.

After the gondolas passed, Sam brought the throttles forward to just a little more than an idle, turning the wheel to the right and taking the next canal. After half a mile, the canal split into two, and at Tom's direction, Sam took the left.

"That's it!" Tom said pointing to a big green door that came right up to the river front. "The Apartments of Saint Maria Formosa."

Sam pulled the boat alongside the jetty at the front and tied up. A doorman told them they couldn't leave the motorboat there unattended.

Tom shrugged. "I'll wait by the car. Give me a yell if you get into trouble."

"All right. But since when have I gotten into trouble?"

"Since when have you not?"

Sam ignored that, clambered out of the boat, and up to the door. The doorman opened the green door and Sam followed a set of internal stairs to level three. At the end of the hallway several police officers lingered.

Sam felt his stomach churn with fear.

A police officer met his eye.

Sam asked, "Is Signore Lorenzo De Luca all right?"

The officer's eyes locked onto him. "I'm sorry, sir, you are?"

"Sam Reilly." He handed the officer his passport.

The officer took it, his eyes darting between the photograph and Sam's face. Seemingly satisfied that the two were matched, the officer said, "How do you know Signore Lorenzo De Luca?"

"I'm afraid I don't. I'm following up on a lead and was hoping he might be able to point me in the right direction."

The policeman raised his eyebrows. "With what?"

"I'm a leading expert on the search and recovery of sunken ships and aircraft. I was brought in to help work on this case with the Phoenix Flight 318." Sam reached into his pocket and retrieved Gerry Emple's card and handed it to the officer. "You can contact this man from the NTSB field office in Catania, he will vouch for me, and can fill you in with what I'm after. Is there any chance I can please talk with Signore Du Luca?"

The officer studied his face, trying to decide whether or not he could be bothered going through the trouble of contacting the NTSB to see if they would corroborate his story. In the end either laziness or Sam's honest face won out, and the officer replied, "I'm afraid that won't be possible."

"Why not?" Sam asked, although he was already pretty certain he knew the answer.

The policeman folded his arms across his chest. "I'm afraid Signore Lorenzo Du Luca has been murdered."

Sam felt the wind disappear from his chest. "Murdered... When?"

"The medical examiner hasn't given us her final report, but she's estimated within the last hour. You don't think the two cases might be connected?"

Sam shook his head. "Unlikely. He was friends with one of the passengers on the flight and I was hoping he could tell me why the man had suddenly booked a flight to Venice."

The officer said, "I suppose now it doesn't matter. You can just ask the passenger himself."

"What do you mean?" Sam asked. "Phoenix Flight 318 hasn't been seen for more than three months!"

"I'm sorry, you didn't hear?"

Sam cocked his eyebrow. "Hear what?"

The officer made a dramatic sigh, as though Sam was wasting his time with trivial news. "Phoenix Flight 318 just landed at Marco Polo International."

CHAPTER THIRTY-NINE

ANDREW GODDARD DIDN'T WAIT AT the carousel to retrieve his luggage.

Instead, he stepped out of the airport and immediately grabbed a water taxi. He'd been trying to reach Lorenzo Du Luca ever since the plane got on the ground. Without an answer, he could only assume the worst — his eternity mask had been compromised.

Worried that someone was following him from the airport, he got the taxi to drop him off at *Saint Marks Square*, where there were more tourists than there was space. He breathed easier as he slipped into the dense crowd.

From there he headed north, navigating the maze of narrow streets and bridges that crossed the ubiquitous canals.

He moved with a determined stride, easily sliding through the hordes of tourists and local Italian workers intending to fleece them. After the events of the last three months there was no way of telling for certain if it was still safe. His gaunt face seemed somehow more withered, as the skin hugged his protracted jaw with defiance. The thought of what would happen if his mask had been taken, sent his heart pounding in his chest.

His cobalt blue eyes searched his surroundings for signs of the upcoming plague. People looked happy, or no more discontent than was normal in modern day life. He exhaled a deep breath of air, oriented himself, and kept moving.

No, he would know by now if THEY had got to his mask.

The whole world would know about it if the Phoenix Plague was released.

The name brought him back to that fateful flight. He knew that boarding an aircraft named after the wretched Phoenix in order to secure the *Homo floresiensis* mask that had been placed on auction was a bad omen.

It didn't matter.

THEY hadn't been able to break him on that damned island. No matter what they tried, he had held out, refusing to reveal the location of his mask.

He crossed the *Rio de San Giovanni Laterano* and stopped.

Behind him, he was certain someone had been following. The person was tall with a solid build, and the determined stride of a professional soldier.

He moved quickly.

Knocking over a small cart on the bridge filled with tacky souvenirs, Goddard started to run. Behind him, the big guy commenced his pursuit.

Goddard was tall and despite his lanky build, he had surprising strength in his legs. He would have made a good sprinter in his youth. He kept running, refusing to look back behind his shoulder, in fear that he might get caught.

He entered the *Basilica Dei Santi Giovanni e Paolo* through the Bartolomeo Bon great west doorway. The enormous brick edifice, designed in the Italian Gothic style, and completed in the 1430s, was the principal Dominican church of Venice, and as such was built to hold large congregations. It is dedicated to

John and Paul, not the Biblical Apostles of the same names, but two obscure martyrs of the Early Christian church in Rome, whose names were recorded in the 4th century but whose legend is of a later date.

Goddard made a quick sign of the cross and made his way toward the east end. The vast interior contained an array of funerary monuments and paintings. On the southern aisle, a number of tourists flocked around the *Madonna della Pace*, a miraculous Byzantine statue situated in its own chapel in the south aisle, and a foot of *Saint Catherine of Siena*, the church's chief relic.

There he walked past a man who was examining the ancient religious relic. The man looked inconspicuous, with a pair of cargo pants and a white shirt. Their eyes locked for a moment and Goddard thought he might have seen some sort of recognition in the man's eyes, which were dark blue like the deepest parts of the ocean.

He broke eye contact and kept walking until he reached a priest at the transept.

The priest was startled by the sight, his eyes widened and his right hand clasped at his crucifix. "Andrew Goddard!"

Goddard dipped his head, his eyes looking at the floor. "I'm sorry father, but it's time."

"I'm about to give mass, can't it wait?'

"No. There are people searching for me even now. I have to take it away from here. You know what's at stake."

"Yes, of course, my son."

The priest led him in toward the end of the sanctuary.

Concealed by the walls of the sanctuary, the priest opened a hatch, revealing a secret set of stairs down into the crypt.

Andrew Goddard took the priest's hand, holding his gaze. "Thank you, father."

"No, thank you, Goddard. God speed."

Andrew quickly climbed down the steep set of spiral stairs.

Beneath the church, he moved quickly, passing the rows of deceased doges who once proffered their wealth on the basilica. At the very end of the crypt, an unnamed vault appeared dull by comparison to that of the wealthy doges.

He carefully wiped back some of the dust that had shrouded the ancient tomb, revealing a small slot, in which to insert a key.

Andrew fumbled with a single brass key attached to a lanyard and held around his neck, removing it to insert in the keyhole.

Once there, he turned it.

The key tensioned, but gave way to the pressure. The internal latches unlocked. He pushed on the side of the vault and was rewarded, when, a moment later, the heavy vault slid open.

He expelled a referent breath of air.

Resting inside was an ancient mask made out of Alexandrite depicting, with the precision of a detailed craftsman, the shape of a *Homo neanderthalensis*.

Goddard didn't stare in awe for very long. He'd never seen the mask in person, but had studied its images for so long that he felt as though he knew the mask intimately.

He picked up the small mask, placed it in his leather bag, and returned to the sanctuary above. Goddard opened the door to step out into the main cathedral and stopped — because there, in front of him was the big guy who'd been following him and the man with the piercing blue eyes.

The shorter of the two men said, "Andrew Goddard?"

Andrew's eyes furtively darted from one man to the other. Both looked dangerous. But the bigger of the two looked positively lethal.

Goddard asked, "What do you want?"

"I think you'd better come with us."

"I'm not going with anyone. This is a house of God, and I expect you to treat it as such, and not spill blood within these walls!"

The shorter of the two men made an incredulous grin. "We're not here to hurt you, Mr. Goddard. We're here to save your life."

Goddard's eyes narrowed. "From what?"

"That I don't know." The shorter man spread his hands. "To be honest, I was hoping you could tell us…"

Andrew felt his heart pounding in the back of his ears.

He had to do something.

But what?

As adrenaline surged in his veins, he pushed through the smaller of the two men, with a level of vehemence that shocked him.

The bigger man reacted fast, trying to grip him by his shoulders, but Goddard twisted and slipped passed him with the speed and efficiency that would make a quarterback smile.

He bolted through the great western door out into *Calle Torelli* and stopped, because he saw a ghost.

Mr. Sneakers — the man from Phoenix Flight 318 — pointed a small handgun at him. "I suggest you come with me, Mr. Goddard."

Andrew followed the man around to the northern side of the basilica. He searched for police, or any passing tourists who might give the madman pause before doing anything irrevocably stupid. But despite being in one of Europe's busiest tourist cities, he found himself surprisingly alone.

"What do you want?"

"You know what I want." The man smiled. There was something sinister, almost reptilian about it. "I want the mask."

Goddard met his smile, with a show of bravado and confidence that surprised himself. "You're going to have to be a little more specific. I'm a fine arts and antiquities dealer — I work with a lot of masks. Is there one in particular you're after?"

"You know I'm talking about the Neanderthal key."

Goddard spread his hands in supplication. "I'm afraid I don't know what you're talking about."

Mr. Sneakers gave a half shrug. "In that case, all I want from you is to die."

A second later, the bell tower's three bells chimed in D major.

And a single shot fired.

CHAPTER FORTY

S AM LAUNCHED HIMSELF AT THE blond-haired assassin.

He collided with the man's shoulder at the same time the man squeezed the trigger of his silenced handgun.

It made a sharp, raspy, sound as the shot fired.

Both men hit the ground hard, knocking the wind out of Sam's lungs.

The shooter tried to squeeze off two more shots in the split second afterward. Sam gripped the man's trigger hand, smashing it against the marble stonework beneath.

The blond-haired man grunted as his knuckles bloodied, but he didn't lose grip of the weapon. Sam swung his fist at the shooter's face, but the man shifted his position with the speed and efficiency of an elite soldier, absorbing the hit on his well-protected, muscular shoulder instead, and using the momentum to roll away quickly. Sam tried to keep hold of the man's wrist, but he yanked it free.

Both men came to a stop three feet away from each other.

Still on the ground, the assassin lined his Glock up, targeting Sam.

Spotting the weapon, and unable to clear the distance in time, Sam rolled out of the way. He gritted his teeth, expecting the life ending blow to follow in an instant.

Instead, Andrew Goddard kicked the Glock with the might of a champion football player. The handgun came free from their attacker's grip, and slid across the marble tiles several feet before falling free, disappearing into the canal below.

The assassin pushed himself off the floor, jumping to a standing position. His eyes darted defiantly between Sam and Goddard, before he opened a flick knife from an unseen pocket. The man grinned as he slashed viciously at Goddard.

Sam shouted, "Tom! Over here..."

Behind him, Tom picked up a four-foot steel temporary fence post, and, gripping it like a baseball bat, he swung the now lethal weapon toward the assassin.

The blond-haired man looked defiant for a moment, and then turned to run.

Andrew Goddard turned to face them. His face reminded Sam of a wizard. He wore his wispy gray hair tidily swept back. Beneath his trim beard, he had an ascetic face, with bony features and a protracted jawline. His intelligent blue eyes met Sam directly, and he smiled warmly.

"Thank you, for saving my life. I'm Andrew Goddard, by the way." The man looked down his long nose at him. "And you are?"

"Sam Reilly." Sam turned to Tom, "And this is Tom Bower."

"Good God!" Goddard said, shaking his head. "What are you doing here?"

Sam cheeks dimpled as he grinned. "Well, actually, I was looking for you."

"Why?"

"Well, to be honest, I wanted to warn you that your life was in danger."

Goddard raised his eyebrows. "Yes, well I think I worked that one out for myself. All the same, I must thank you both again for saving my life."

Sam said, "If it's all the same to you, I think we'd better get out of here, before your friend tries to rectify that."

Goddard turned his gaze in the direction that their attacker had run off. "Agreed."

All three of them climbed onto the wooden motor boat and Tom switched it on, starting the powerful V8 engine.

Sam removed the bow line and pushed off from the jetty.

Goddard said, "You'll have to fill me in on how you knew I was in danger."

"And you'll have to fill me in on how you know who I am?" Sam said. "But I'm afraid that's all going to have to wait, because we have company…"

CHAPTER FORTY-ONE

T HE MACHINEGUN BULLETS RAKED THE water just ten feet away.
Sam and Goddard ducked to the floor, as Tom gunned the throttle, and the motorboat raced ahead east along *Rio de Santa Marina*. Their boat lifted up onto the aquaplane within seconds as it skimmed along the narrow canal.

Edging his eyes above the wooden stern, Sam spotted the boat in pursuit. It looked more like a predator than a pleasure craft. It had sharp lines, angled in various directions and was covered in matte black paint like a stealth fighter jet. The sports boat's twin engines made a deafening roar, as its skipper worked to close the gap.

Tom swung the motorboat to the right, into *Rio de la Tetta*.

Sam braced his back against the leather seat behind him, and started removing the leather cover from the seat ahead, throwing everything and anything in his way over his shoulder.

Behind them, the stealth boat narrowed the gap.

Two people were now firing at them.

"You'd better hurry, Sam!" Tom shouted. "I can't keep ahead of them for much longer."

"I'm working on it!"

"Great… if you could work faster…"

"I'll try."

Sam cursed and threw a series of oily rags, and mechanical tools out from the storage compartment, to reveal an empty container.

Sam shouted, "It's not there!"

Tom shrugged. "Try the portside!"

"What are you looking for?" Goddard asked.

Sam, focused on his task at hand, ignored the question, and quickly popped the wooden latches to the portside storage compartment.

It opened first go, revealing an M24 bolt-action 7.62×51mm Sniper Rifle.

Goddard's jaw opened and his cobalt blue eyes widened. "For God's sake, if you had a sniper rifle all this time, why didn't you take it with you before!"

Sam opened the bipod, mounting it onto the wooden stern. "It's not exactly the most secretive device to carry. Besides, do you really suggest I should bring a sniper rifle into a cathedral?"

"Perhaps a small weapon, like a Berretta would have been more the thing?"

"I'm sure it would have been, but recent anti-terrorism laws, have introduced metal detectors throughout parts of Venice. Besides, if you thought your life was in danger, why didn't you think of it?"

"At sixty-one, I thought my days of playing Indiana Jones were over…"

Tom shouted, "Duck!"

The motorboat swung round a sharp bend into *Rio de San Zulan* beneath a shallow bridge. On the other side, Tom gunned the engine, and the boat quickly came alive onto the aquaplane. A small group of gondolas made their way along the narrow river.

"Out of the way!" Tom yelled, as he swerved to the left of them.

The sniper rifle slid out of its position onto the floor.

Sam swore, as he picked it up again, setting it back on its bipod mount.

Behind them, the bigger stealth boat raced through, causing the tourists and gondoliers to jump from their gondolas. An instant later, the stealth boat slammed through the gondolas, sending them flying into the air in shards of splintered wood.

Sam loaded the *7.62×51mm NATO* shot into the chamber, and stared down the telescopic sight. He eyed the skipper at the wheel, and squeezed the trigger.

The shot splintered the fiberglass hull to the right of the skipper, but it was enough to give the man pause.

Tom followed the river round in a large u-shape.

Sam asked, "You know where you're going?"

"No!"

His eyes turned to Goddard. "What about you?"

Goddard glanced at his surroundings, recognition filling his eyes. "Yes. Where are you trying to get to?"

"Out of here. Fastest route possible."

Goddard squinted, then moving up ahead, toward Tom, he said, "Take this left."

Tom took the left, swerving past another gondola.

At the end of the canal it opened up to a much wider river.

"Go right!" Goddard said. "This is the *Grand Canal*."

Clear from the constraints of the narrow canals, Tom opened up the throttles, and the motorboat raced ahead.

Sam expelled a deep breath of air as they tore away with the breeze in his hair, as every second took them farther away from their attackers. Nearly at the mouth of the *Grand Canal* Sam could practically taste freedom on the horizon.

Round the next bend, they came face to face with the black stealth boat.

Tom swerved to the right down *Rio de Noale*, sending a sharp bow wave in an ever-expanding arc, across the *Grand Canal*.

The stealth boat must have circled around on the outside of the *Venetian Lagoon* — or they had a second vessel — either way, it meant they were dealing with a well-funded, well-equipped, and well-orchestrated team of mercenaries.

The *Rio de Noale* was a particularly narrow canal that cut through the bulk of Venice in a straight line out to the *Isola di San Michele* — an island cemetery.

Being in a straight canal, Tom was able to bring the boat up to its maximum speed, but it was going to do nothing to help them escape. They already knew it was impossible to escape the faster motorboat.

"I can't outrun them!" Tom said, "You got a plan?"

"I'm working on it," Sam said, through gritted teeth.

He fumbled with a yellow twenty-gallon reserve fuel container, and EPA be damned, he dropped it over the stern.

The yellow container bobbed up and down on the surface of the water in the middle of the canal.

Sam placed his eye up to the sniper rifle's telescopic scope.

Through his right eye he lined the crosshairs up with the gasoline container. He blinked, and his left eye spotted the stealth boat as it raced into the canal.

He squeezed the trigger.

The shot struck the fuel container.

It sparked, causing the gasoline to light up in a giant ball of fire.

A torrent of heat burst through the narrow confines of the canal, hitting the stealth boat head on. The boat ploughed through the flames and flipped upside down, where its momentum dragged it forward, smashing into the pontoon of a masonry bridge—sending its fiberglass hull splintering into hundreds of fractured pieces.

Tom eased off the throttle, taking their speed to a more survivable pace, and came out the opposite end of *Rio de Noale*. Back in the open waters of the outer lagoon, he opened the throttles fully, and they raced toward the Marco Polo International Airport.

Goddard said, "Well, I think that got rid of them this time."

"I'd say so." Sam grinned. "Now do you want to tell me why someone went to the trouble of stealing an entire passenger jet just to get to you—and for that matter, why you should be so surprised that I of all people have turned up to protect you?"

Goddard opened his mouth to speak, turned his head to gaze back at *Campanile di San Marco*, the bell tower, and highest point in Venice, and then said, "What do you know about the *Eternity Masks*?"

CHAPTER FORTY-TWO

S AM SEARCHED HIS MENTAL MEMORY banks for the reference, but was coming up blank. "Nothing. Why? What should I know?"

"I don't know. I thought, given your knowledge of the Master Builders, you might have heard about them."

The Master Builders were an ancient race of highly intelligent people who Sam believed helped design and build some of the greatest engineering feats on Earth, including the great pyramids. Most archeologists dismissed his theory as being fanciful at best.

Sam's lips curled into a wry smile. "What do you know about the Master Builders?"

"I know enough," Goddard said, his voice in a tone that inflected he didn't need to be questioned further on his knowledge. "I know that you've spent years trying to prove their existence."

Sam wanted to know more about how Goddard knew about the Master Builders, but realized he wasn't going to get anything yet. Instead, he asked, "How do the Master Builders fit in with the *Eternity Masks*?"

Goddard's gaze returned from the now distant skyline of Venice, landing directly on Sam's searching eyes. "Everything. It has everything to do with the Master Builders."

Sam smiled. "So, are you going to fill us in, or should we just drop you off at the wharf and we'll go our separate ways?"

Goddard ignored his quip. "Do you know how many relatively intelligent bipeds sharing the genus of *Homo* roamed the Earth up until a hundred thousand years ago?"

"Seven," Sam replied without hesitation, meeting Goddard's eye. "In addition to Homo sapiens, there were still Homo erectus, Homo floresiensis, Homo habilis, Homo heidelbergensis, Homo naledi, and Homo neanderthalensis."

Goddard laughed. "Well done. Good to see you were paying attention, somewhere along the way."

Sam was starting to see what this was all about, but he asked, "Seven subspecies of human, reduced to just one, *Homo-sapiens* — the most successful, albeit most destructive of the lot."

"Right."

Sam sighed, waiting for him to continue.

Goddard's eyes drifted toward the *San Giuliano* bridge, and then said, "Given what we know about the human race, how do you think seven subspecies of humans would have fared if they were still alive today?"

Nearly eight billion *Homo sapiens* are probably enough for the world. "Poorly."

"Exactly. That's what the ancient Master Builders thought."

"The Master Builders wiped out the other six sub-species of human?"

Goddard crossed his arms. "No. I'm afraid we did that ourselves without their help."

"Then what?"

"The Master Builders gave us the *Eternity Masks*." Goddard

searched Sam's face for recognition, finding none, he continued. "The Master Builders knew that the world couldn't sustain all seven. Legend goes that they devised a plan to make the two most successful species thrive, taking their rightful position on the top of the evolutionary ladder."

Sam asked, "What was supposed to happen to the other species?"

"I don't know, but I guess they expected them to become extinct, or simply accept a lower position in the intelligence chain — think about apes that were smart enough to perform complex tasks."

"Like a slave race?"

Goddard spread his hands and shrugged. "Hey I didn't make the rules."

The Master Builders were setting up a game of wits. The winners won the divine right to live. The losers, became extinct, or submitted to slavery.

Sam rolled the concept around in the back of his mind.

It made sense to him.

The Master Builders, although human, had a genetic disorder that prevented their telomeres from shortening, and as a consequence, lived exceptionally long lives, in excess of three hundred or more years. They were used to being smarter than those around them, more powerful, and treated like Gods.

Sam took a deep breath. "How did it work?"

"The Master Builders forged seven different masks. Within each was stored a very precise code in the form of weight, individual materials used, and conductivity. Each mask could be used as an individual key to unlock an ancient vault of knowledge. It takes two keys, a combination of any two of them, to open the chamber door."

Sam arched his eyebrow. "The Master Builders wanted us to work together?"

Goddard nodded. "It would appear so."

"But not all seven species?"

"No. I believe they had the foresight to understand that was never possible."

"So why two? Why not three or four… or, simply one — *Homo sapiens*?"

"I've given this some thought over the years…" Goddard steepled his long, bony fingers, his eyes staring in the distance. "Do you know that more than two percent of today's population has some Neanderthal DNA?"

Sam nodded. "Yes, but I didn't know it was that high."

"I wonder if the ancient Master Builders, assuming they did indeed have a plan, hoped to blend two species together to make a more efficient species."

"It's a definite possibility, but while we're going down that path, why not assume that they wanted all seven species to genetically merge?"

Goddard laughed. When he stopped he looked down his long nose, over his spectacles and fixed his blue eyes on Sam. "What's to say that it hasn't?"

Sam realized this line of reasoning could easily go on for days. Returning to the problem at hand, he asked, "So if the leaders — or whatever one wanted to call the brightest minds at the time roughly a hundred thousand years ago — were told that all they needed to do was acquire two or more keys and they would be granted access to the most extraordinary horde of knowledge, and the power that such a thing brings, why didn't they?"

"Why didn't they simply get along with each other so that they could open the vault?" Goddard's lips formed a condescending smile. "Have you learnt nothing about the human race?"

"No, I'm saying, what have they been doing in the last hundred thousand years? I mean, you take any other form of wealth, such as gold for an example. People simply take it. Wars are fought, religions form to gather it, people are betrayed — somehow, in one way or another, I find it impossible to believe that one species simply never managed to get control of the two masks."

"Ah, I see what you mean now." Goddard nodded, looking, to Sam at least, more and more like an erudite wizard about to enlighten him. "You see, the Master Builders, in their infinite wisdom, decided to bury each mask in a different location around the globe, so that as the species evolved, and became more industrialized, they would discover the masks."

Sam started to see it now, the fog of mystery finally lifting its haze. "How many masks have been found?"

Goddard set his jaw. "Until recently, only one. The *Homo sapiens* mask. The one that I possess and must protect for all our sake."

Sam knew that Sandi Larson hadn't told anyone about the mask yet. "You said, until recently... what's changed?"

"Three months ago, I received an urgent message. Someone in Venice had died and all of his varied possessions were to be auctioned. One of those items was a *Homo naledi* mask. By the time I received the message, there was only one flight to take to reach Venice in time — thus someone forced me to board Phoenix Airlines Flight 318."

"What are you saying... you were tricked into boarding that flight specifically, with a fake *Eternity Mask*?"

Goddard nodded. "I was tricked all right, there was no auction — the collector who had apparently died never even existed, but the *Homo naledi* mask was real."

"How do you know that?"

"Because I've seen an image of all seven masks."

"Really? How did that happen?"

"My father took a photo of all seven of them — actually, paintings of them displayed on a wall in a cave where he found the mask, back in 1925. He actually took a photograph with what was considered the quite revolutionary Leitz camera. The photos are black and white and of a poor quality. But the shapes are indisputable."

"Do you have a copy of the photograph?"

Goddard pulled up his smartphone, searched his image folders, and handed it to him. "Here, have a look at this. In the cave where my father took it, he said the entire wall had a strange purple hue to it."

Sam took the cell phone and stared at the image.

It was identical to the one that he'd developed from a Kodak 620 Duo camera found in the cockpit of what appeared to be Amelia Earhart's Electra.

"Has anyone else seen this?" Sam asked.

"No one who's still alive. My father died years ago, and my back up plan was for Lorenzo De Luca to inherit the mask—and with it, my problem."

Sam said, "Therefore, whoever set you up with the *Homo naledi* mask was the real deal. They know about the game, and they're willing to stop at nothing to get it."

"That's what I'm worried about. Even though we're down to just the human race, there's nothing to stop someone ruthlessly stealing the information from the ancient chamber—and with that sort of power, who knows what they're capable of."

"Of course... whoever's responsible has some serious financial backing to be capable of hijacking a passenger plane and then return it in three months..." Sam stopped.

Goddard met his face. "What is it?"

"I just thought of something..."

"What?"

"How did THEY know that you were going to be on that flight?"

Goddard shuffled in his seat. "Oh, that's easy. They sent me a link to the auction in Venice with a picture of the *Homo naledi* mask."

"No, no… I get that. What I'm trying to work out, is how did they know that you had the *Homo neanderthalensis* mask? And for that matter that you were in New York at the time?"

Goddard licked his dry lips. His face reddened. He expelled a small breath. "Look. In that respect I played into their plans like a fool."

"How?"

"The *Homo naledi* mask wasn't the first fake auction they'd set up."

"It wasn't?"

"No. They had one depicting a *Homo sapiens* mask being auctioned in New York. It was well advertised around the world. They gave plenty of time, so that anyone who knew about the mask would immediately recognize it. There were about sixty people who flew into New York specifically to buy that mask. Sixty possible candidates."

Sam said, "Go on."

"The auction finished at 3:25 p.m. Ten minutes later, someone came into the room and advised that there was a similar mask, this one depicting a *Homo floresiensis*. By the time I had called the airlines company to try and find a flight, Phoenix Airlines Flight 318 was the only one available. In retrospect, I see now that THEY had used a sieving technique to get everyone and anyone who knew anything about the seven sacred masks on that flight. They had no way of knowing who knew something and more importantly, who had one of the remaining six masks."

Sam was intrigued. "How did they get control of the plane?"

Goddard closed his eyes, as though he was back on the plane. The lines around his face deepened and darkened. "THEY drugged us. Something in the ventilation system I'd guess. There was a strong and sweet taste in the air. At first, I thought it was the cognac I'd had, but looking back on it now, I suppose it could have been some sort of ether—they use that in anesthetics, don't they?"

Sam nodded. "I believe so."

"When I woke up, I saw everyone around me was unconscious. Not just around me, but on the plane. I was the only one awake. I stumbled around as though I were still in a dream for some time. In fact, I was almost certain I was having a nightmare." Tears welled in Goddard's eyes, and he took a moment to wipe them away with a handkerchief. "By the time I realized I was awake and something terrible had caused everyone else to be unconscious, I made my way up to the cockpit only to discover the pilots weren't there. I tried to mayday for help, but no one would listen to me, they just kept telling me that the plane I purported to be on, had crashed three days earlier and the wreckage was found with no survivors."

"Any idea why you woke up first?"

Goddard nodded. "I've given this a lot of thought over the last three months. I have a third kidney. It's a genetic abnormality. It's not common, but then it's regular enough that I wasn't the first person my doctor had met with the condition. One of the side effects means that my body metabolizes and excretes toxins — aka anesthetic drugs — faster."

"What happened to the plane?"

"I stepped out of the cockpit, and found that now all the passengers were missing. I kind of lost my mind, ran around the cabin, screaming in a sort of delirium filled rage. When I tried to return to the cockpit, the door was closed and locked. Inside, a man was at the controls. I screamed at him, but when he turned around to face me, he put his finger to his lips as if to tell me to be quiet, in case I wake the other passengers."

"Who would have the power to orchestrate something like this?"

Even as Sam said the words, his mind returned to the CIA director and Chairman of the Joint Chiefs of Staff he saw speaking to each other at the Pentagon.

And he remembered the words the Secretary of Defense recently warned him about…

We have a traitor in the Pentagon.

Sam said, "All right. Do you know where the entrance to the ancient chamber is?"

"Not exactly. I know it's hidden in Malta somewhere. I've made up a list of ancient megalithic structures where it could be buried beneath. We'll know more once we have a second mask."

"Why?"

"The masks are magnetized. Only, unlike a compass, they point toward the hidden chamber from the place where they were found. The problem is, that with only one mask, all I can do is see that the mask points toward Malta."

"Why not Russia? It would be on the same line."

"That's always a possibility, but I don't think so. Anyway, it doesn't matter. With a second mask we can use each mask to draw an imaginary line through Malta. Wherever they intersect is our place."

Sam said, "One thing's for certain. We can't let whoever THEY are beat us to the ancient chamber of knowledge."

Goddard shook his head. "It doesn't matter. With only one mask, there's no point. The mask is merely ornamental on its own."

"How many do you need to access the vault?"

"Two."

"Just two?" Sam sounded hopeful.

"It's one more than we have." Goddard made a hopeful smile. "Unless you happen to have one?"

Sam grinned. "As a matter of fact, I do."

CHAPTER FORTY-THREE

Grand Harbor, Malta

T HE *MOONLIGHT SONATA*, ROUNDED THE large, isolated
breakwater at *Ricasoli Point*, and turned west into the northeast facing mouth of the Grand Harbor at six a.m. The sun of
first light struck the masonry walls of *Fort Saint Elmo* turning
them into a bright gold. The fort looked indestructible, a tribute
to the Maltese strength, endurance, and solidarity during times
of the crucible of war—of which there had been many over the
years.

The 190-foot luxury pleasure cruiser reduced its engines to
idle, and coasted into the Grand Harbor. It shrank beneath the
majestic masonry walls, which had been used since the
Phoenician times. The stilled water appeared a mixed shade of
blues, purples, and reds in the dawn light. Sam Reilly's eyes
swept the harbor's landscape with delight. It was one of the
greatest harbors in the world, and for such a small country, it
had sent very large ripples that changed the course of history
throughout Europe.

The name Malta itself came from the Phoenician word "Maltae," meaning a sheltered anchorage. The Grand Harbor was a wide stretch of water separating the capital city of *Valletta* from the historic towns of *Three Cities*. The harbor has been a hive of activity for over two thousand years. Despite being just over 122 square miles, Malta has wielded enormous influence over the history of Europe, the greatest being during the Great Siege of Malta.

On May eighteen, 1565 the small island country was attacked by a Turkish armada, which set sail from Constantinople on March twenty-two, and was by all accounts, one of the largest assembled since antiquity. During the siege, a group of roughly 9,000 defenders—consisting of the Maltese Knights of St. John, foreign soldiers from Italy, Spain, and Greece, and six thousand civilians—held the city, defeating a Turkish armada of 45,000 on board 131 galleys, 7 galliots, 4 galleasses, and more than forty transport vessels.

Malta lost a third of its population, but it had managed to withstand a siege of more than four months, which ultimately turned the tide in Europe. This led to the end of the Ottoman Empire, Europe's most powerful empire at the time.

Jean de Valette, Grand Master of the Knights of Malta, had a key influence in the victory against the Ottomans with his example and his ability to encourage and hold people together. This example had a major impact, bringing together the kings of Europe in an alliance against the previously seemingly invincible Ottomans; the result was the vast union of forces against the Ottomans at the Battle of Lepanto seven years later. The gratitude of Europe for the knights' heroic defense was so great that money soon began pouring into the island, allowing de Valette to construct a fortified city, Valletta, on Mt. Sciberras.

As the *Moonlight Sonata* continued toward the Port Authority, Sam thought about Valletta's many titles, recalling its rich historical past. It was considered a modern city built by the Knights of St. John, a masterpiece of the Baroque, a European

Art City and a World Heritage City. Ruled successively by the Phoenicians, Greeks, Carthaginians, Romans, Byzantines, Arabs and the Order of the Knights of St. John, and finally the British before gaining its own sovereignty, it is one of the most concentrated historic areas in the world. The Grand Harbor was the base for the Knights of St. John for 268 years, and after their departure became a strategic base for the British for a further 170 years.

And now, it was to become home to the *Ancient Chamber of Human Knowledge,* the oldest human-built structure on Earth, and supposedly a receptacle of all knowledge acquired throughout human evolution — capable of empowering all those who reach it.

The *Moonlight Sonata*'s twin propellers were shifted into reverse, and the throttles opened with a short burst, causing the pleasure cruiser to come to a complete stop in the water.

Sam Reilly zipped up his dry bag, stepped toward Pauline, embraced her for a moment, and gave her a kiss on her cheek. "Thanks for this. I'll make it up to you one day."

She pulled back, squeezing his hand tenderly. "You'd better. I'm going to have some serious trouble explaining this one away if the owner happens to check out where his yacht is tracking on GPS."

Sam spread his palms skyward. "Just tell him you were trying to save the world."

She nodded. "Goodbye, Sam."

"Goodbye, Pauline."

Goddard finished zipping up his wetsuit and pulled his buoyancy control device across his shoulders, attaching the Velcro onto his waist. "Are you sure this is necessary?"

Sam shrugged. "Hey, I had a perfectly good private jet waiting for me at Marco Polo International. You're the one who suggested we had better enter Malta unannounced, and off custom's radar, in case our enemies followed."

"What do we do when we get to the other side?"

"I have a friend who lives nearby. He's agreed to lend us a vehicle and a place to stay where he lives with his family in *Marsa.*"

"All right, let's get this over and done with."

Sam checked Goddard's SCUBA set up, testing the regulator, dive gauge, and BCD. "You've dived before, right?"

"Sure. About thirty years ago, in the Bahamas, mind you. But I'm told it's very much like riding a bicycle."

Sam grinned. "That it is. Just keep breathing."

"Good advice. I'll follow you."

Sam placed the regulator into his mouth, and stepped off the back of the yacht, disappearing into the deep waters below.

CHAPTER FORTY-FOUR

SAM SURFACED AT THE SITE of the former Malta Tram Station in Marsa.

It was an industrial shipping area, with dozens of shipyards nearby, where people worked on, in, and under many large shipping vessels. If anyone was watching, they would have assumed he and Goddard were just working under one of the hulls, most likely freeing it from barnacles to save the ships being slipped.

Sam removed his fins and dive mask, climbed up the ladder at the side of the harbor, and moved with the confident and purposeful gait of someone who belonged, across the road and into a small park. Goddard followed behind quickly.

They both stripped from their wetsuits, changing into a comfortable pair of cargo shorts, Italian name brand polo shirts, and a pair of Birkenstock leather sandals, giving them the appearance of wealthy tourists. They left their SCUBA equipment next to a nearby bin, in the zipped-up bag.

Goddard's eyes drifted toward the unlikely rubbish. "You're just going to dump them?"

"No, it's okay, my friend said he'll come pick them up this afternoon."

"Great. Where now?"

"My friend's house. He lives up the road."

They walked along the narrow streets for a few blocks, traveling the old paved roads that had lasted more than a thousand years, until they reached a three-story terrace, in a row of twelve.

Sam knocked on the door.

A man opened it and smiled at him warmly. He looked like he belonged in an oil painting during the Renaissance. His pale blue eyes were set as though he was dreaming. He had a handsome face that looked like it was almost chiseled, with a jaw line that betrayed no hint of fat, a firm chin and a straight patriarchal nose. His dark beard was perfectly manicured, and he wore a pair of diamond studded earrings.

"Sam Reilly!" The man leaned in to embrace him with a firm handshake and a big hug.

"It's great to see you. It's been too long." Afterward, Sam turned to Goddard. "Andrew, I'd you to meet my cousin, Emmanuel Azzopardi."

"Pleased to meet you," Goddard said, offering his hand.

Emmanuel opened the door and stepped to the side. Using his hand to gesture them in, he said, "Come in, come in. Can I offer you a drink? Have you eaten?"

"We're good, my cousin," Sam said, closing the door behind him. "Look. We've got to get around Malta pretty quickly. There is something really important we have to do. You said that you had a vehicle I could borrow?"

"Of course. It's around the back, in the garage. Do you have time to wait until Christine gets home? I'm sure she and the kids would love to see you."

Sam made a half-frown. "Afraid not. We've got to get going and the less people who know we're here the better. Like I said before, we're in trouble. Some dangerous people are after us."

"Okay. I understand. Take whatever you need and know that you have a place here to sleep if you want it." Emmanuel made a wry smile. "If I didn't know you better, I'd start to think you'd gotten yourself in with the wrong crowd."

Sam gripped his hand with a firm shake. "Thanks. I'll make it up to you once this is all over."

"I know you will," Emmanuel said, sagely. "Good luck."

Sam followed him round the back of the old masonry house, and through a door into the single car garage.

Parked there in the middle, was a blue BMW R1200 sports motorcycle.

Sam grinned. "This is what you're lending me?"

Emmanuel nodded. "Yes. I assume you can still ride a motorcycle?"

CHAPTER FORTY-FIVE

T HE FERRY DROPPED THEM OFF on the island of Gozo in the north.

As the disembarking ramp lowered, Sam placed the open face helmet on his head, tightened the strap and got onto the front of the motorcycle. He pressed the starter button and Goddard climbed on the back, still carrying his precious *Homo sapiens* mask in a backpack.

The traffic light ahead turned green and Sam rode off the boat, following the rest of the vehicles until he reached the main road. Then he gunned the throttle, taking off ahead of everyone.

Goddard had explained to him that he'd narrowed the location down to somewhere in Malta, but as yet hadn't been able to narrow it down further. Instead, he had created a list of ancient temples, which he believed may have been constructed in honor of the ancient *Chamber of Knowledge*. That list, he again shortened to just two ancient temples — Xagħra Hypogeum on Gozo and Ħal-Saflieni Hypogeum on mainland Malta.

His theory was that over the course of history, the ancient chamber had become buried with antiquity, including all reference to the lost knowledge. Their hope today was that Sam Reilly, with his unique knowledge of the Master Builders might find something on one of the ancient temples that Goddard had missed. Sandi Larson would meet them tomorrow with the *Homo neanderthalensis* mask and together, the three of them would hopefully reveal the Master Builder's most sacred secret.

The Xagħra Hypogeum on Gozo was the first place on the list.

Sam pulled the BMW motorcycle around the front of the ancient complex. The Neolithic funerary complex consisted of a series of underground caves which were used to bury the dead inside a walled hypogeum. It mainly dated back to around 3000 to 2400 BC, although the earliest tombs at the site date back to 4100 to 3800 BC. The caves collapsed sometime before 2000 BC, and the site was later used for domestic and agricultural purposes.

They walked around the remains of the Xagħra Stone Circle, which originally consisted of a walled enclosure surrounding underground caves which were used as a necropolis. It had some similarities to the Hypogeum of Ħal-Saflieni, a prehistoric funerary complex on the main island of Malta. Uniquely, excavations at the site showed that the bodies of the deceased were dismembered, and the different body parts were buried at separate places.

Sam examined the stone walls. They were made out of soft limestone. No sign of the dark, glassy obsidian with which he knew the Master Builders were capable of manipulating and building. Nearby there were the fractured remnants of a number of ancient temples ranging between 4100 and 3800 BC, during the Żebbuġ phase of Maltese prehistory—but none of those appeared to show any Master Builder influence.

An hour later, Sam noticed that Goddard had gone for a little walk to the end of the collapsed cave system. He followed him. The older man was leaning deep into a small opening that had formed between two large stone pillars, leaving only his legs visible from the outside.

Sam's eyes narrowed, trying to work out what he was doing. It looked impossible for him to fit any farther inside. A moment later, Goddard pushed himself out.

Sam smiled. "Find anything?"

Goddard shook his head, his eyes somewhat furtive, darted away. "There have been some heavy rains since I was last here. It looks like it's eroded a small opening just here. I hoped that maybe it would lead to a lower level."

"Did it?"

"No. Just another dead end." Goddard brightened up. "What about you? Did you find anything?"

Sam's eyes drifted lazily down the hill toward the blue sea. He shook his head. "It wasn't here."

Goddard's eyes narrowed. "You're sure?"

"Certain. There's always the chance that whoever built this structure did so directly on top of the much more ancient *Chamber of Knowledge,* but it definitely wasn't the Master Builders."

"All right, let's go. Maybe we'll have better luck at the Hypogeum of Ħal-Saflieni."

"Agreed."

They caught the afternoon ferry, and didn't get to the Hypogeum of Ħal-Saflieni in Paola until the early evening. Sam Reilly knew one of the archeologists who had worked on the site, who agreed to open it up to them outside of the normal tour times.

The Neolithic subterranean structure dated back to the Saflieni phase—somewhere between 3300—3000 BC—in Maltese prehistory. The underground structure was thought to have been a sanctuary and necropolis, with the remains of more than 7,000 individuals documented by archeologists. The Hypogeum was discovered by accident in 1902 when workers cutting cisterns for a new housing development broke through its roof. The workers, fearing loss of construction work in the area, tried to hide the temple at first, but eventually it was found, and an archeology search was conducted.

Sam introduced Goddard to his friend, Jen Potter, who then led them in through the upper levels of the museum and down into the Hypogeum.

It was constructed entirely underground and consisted of three superimposed levels hewn into soft globigerina limestone, with its halls and chambers interconnected through a labyrinthine series of steps, lintels and doorways.

Jen said, "The upper level is thought to have been occupied first, with the middle and lower levels expanded and excavated later. Some of the middle chambers appear to share stylistic characteristics with the contemporaneous Megalithic Temples found across Malta."

Sam ran his eyes across the limestone walls. "Was any obsidian ever found during the excavation?"

Jen thought about that for a moment. "Actually, there was. Crude tools including antlers, flint, chert, and obsidian were strewn throughout the cave system."

"But none of the chambers were ever carved in obsidian?"

"No. Malta itself is almost entirely globigerina limestone. We don't have any obsidian caves."

Sam nodded. "Okay."

They continued down into the first level, which had multiple rooms of individual and expanded caves. The second level was apparently a later expansion, with the rock hoisted up to the surface by Cyclopean rigging.

The middle level consisted of four unique rooms.

With a flashlight in his hand, he followed Jen into the main chamber. The main chamber was roughly circular and carved out from the limestone rock. A number of trilithon entrances were represented, some blind, and others leading to another chamber. Sam noticed that most of the wall surfaces had received a red wash of ochre.

Jen said, "It was in here that the *Sleeping Lady* was recovered."

Sam frowned. "The *Sleeping Lady*?"

"Yes, when archeologists first entered this room, they found a small stone figurine. It's now housed in the Museum of Archaeology, in Valletta."

Sam and Goddard followed her through to the Oracle Room.

It was vaguely shaped like a rectangle. Running the beam of his flashlight across the walls and roof, Sam noticed the room had an elaborately painted ceiling, consisting of spirals in red ochre with circular spots.

Sam asked, "Why do they call it the Oracle Room?"

His voice echoed.

"It has to do with the peculiar acoustic resonance from any vocalization made inside." Jen's voice echoed as she spoke. "See?"

"Interesting."

They turned left and entered a spacious hall, with circular, inward slanting walls, richly decorated in geometrical patterns of spirals. He flicked the beam of his flashlight around the vaulted room, stopping on the far-right side of the wall, near the entrance, where a petrosomatoglyph of a human hand was carved into the wall.

Goddard stared at the hand. "Does that have any specific relevance to the Master Builders?"

Sam shook his head. "No. Not that I've seen before."

They turned left and entered the Holy of Holies.

The vault was the most central structure of the Hypogeum. According to Jen, the room was perfectly oriented toward the winter solstice, which would have illuminated its façade from the original opening, some six thousand years earlier.

Sam ran his eyes across the unique structure.

The focal point was a porthole within a trilithon — a structure consisting of two large vertical stones–which in turn was framed within a larger trilithon and yet another even larger trilithon. The corbelled ceiling matched with archeological recreations of the Megalithic temples found throughout Malta's surface landscape.

Jen caught Sam's eye. "Find what you were looking for?"

"I don't think so, but the Hypogeum's fascinating, nonetheless." His eyes landed on a small wooden grate that protected people from falling down a vertical shaft. "Where does that lead?"

"Down into an empty storage chamber."

"Does it lead anywhere?"

"No. The entire place has been mapped using lasers. Why?"

Sam crunched his face together. "We're looking for an even older temple. We were hoping that maybe the Hypogeum was built on top of it. Any chance of a vault buried deeper?"

"No. Ground penetrating radar has been used. The Hypogeum ends there."

Goddard looked at Sam. "What are you thinking?"

"It's an amazing place, but I doubt very much that the Master Builders were involved in its construction."

Jen said, "You have a theory that this place you're looking for was protected by an ancient temple?"

Sam nodded. "Yeah. Think of an ancient cult, sworn to protect it. When they die out, the last person might try and pass the role onto the next generation. Religions change; things are buried, and only the best stories are passed down through the ages like legends. What we're looking for is much more than six thousand years old."

"If you're looking for something like that, why stop at the Megalithic temples and Hypogeums?"

"Well," Sam said. "What we're looking for is probably the oldest man-made structure in Malta, so we needed to start with the oldest temples. Why? Do you have a better idea?"

"Yeah. Why restrict yourselves to Megalithic temples?" Jen glanced at him, judging his reaction. "What about a Catholic church."

Sam and Goddard simultaneously dismissed the idea. "Too young."

"Ah, but some of the great churches throughout Malta were built on top of ancient Megalithic temples."

"Really?" Sam's lips curled into a smile. "I didn't know that. Why?"

"Probably for the same reason the temples were built there in the first place — they shared the best locations, a high point, a specific position in relation to the sun, or the most defensive landscape." She made a small laugh. "That and, hey the island was riddled with Megalithic temples, so it was only a matter of time before our multitude of churches had to coincide with the same locations."

"That's a good idea," Sam said, "Thanks we'll give it a look."

Jen asked, "Anything else unique about this buried vault that you're looking for?"

Sam turned to Goddard. "Anything you can think of?"

Goddard thought about that for a moment. "I suppose it might be buried beneath a younger temple, such as a church, which was built over the top of it."

"That means we're back to the drawing board. Where do you want to begin?" Sam said.

"Let's look at churches," Goddard suggested.

"That shouldn't be hard," Jen said. "Malta, despite being small, has probably more churches than any other country on Earth."

Sam thought about that for a moment. "Okay, let's narrow the field."

Goddard asked, "How?"

Sam glanced at a map of Malta. "You said that the masks are

drawn to Malta by some sort of unexplained magnetic field?"

Goddard said, "That's right. I can't say for certain the second one does, but mine certain did."

Sam said, "So, let's see if there are any churches that have any involvement in events that couldn't be explained away with science?"

Jen said, "Like what, miracles?"

Sam grinned. "You're right. Miracles, exactly!"

"What?" Goddard asked.

Sam said, "I think I know where the Chamber of Knowledge is buried."

CHAPTER FORTY-SIX

Shangri La Hotel, Malta

R HYSE VAUGHN PICKED UP HIS cell phone and dialed an international number by heart.

A curt voice answered. "I said not to contact me on this number. It's not safe."

Rhyse said, "I've lost him!"

The cell phone went silent, and for a second, he thought the man had hung up on him.

General Painter's voice came back in a whisper. "Ah, shit... what happened?"

"He got away with the Mask in Venice. He had help from Sam Reilly and his big friend, what's his name?"

"Tom Bower?"

"That's the one." Rhyse said, "They lost us. I sent a man to follow Reilly's private plane, which flew from Venice to Paris, but only Tom Bower got off."

"Where's the jet now?"

"Still sitting on the tarmac in Paris."

"Where are you now?"

"Malta."

"Surely it hasn't come to that yet?"

Rhyse said, "I don't know. According to customs, Reilly and Goddard haven't entered the country. But that doesn't mean they're not here."

"What are you going to do?"

Rhyse opened the briefcase. It was loaded with C4. He pressed the arm button next to the timer and closed the lid. "I'm going to go wait by the church… in case they turn up."

CHAPTER FORTY-SEVEN

Basilica of the Assumption of our Lady, Malta

S AM REILLY STARED UP AT the massive Basilica.

The design of the present church is based on the Pantheon in Rome, and at one point had the third largest unsupported dome in the world. It was built between 1833 and the 1860s to Neoclassical designs of Giorgio Grognet de Vassé, on the site of an earlier Renaissance church which had been built around 1614 to designs of Tommaso Dingli.

But was there an even older church?

At 4:40 p.m. on April 9, 1942, the Luftwaffe dropped three bombs on the church, and two of them deflected without exploding. However, a third one, an eleven-hundred-pound high explosive bomb pierced the dome and entered the church, where a congregation of more than three hundred people were awaiting early evening mass.

The bomb didn't explode. This event was interpreted by the Maltese as a miracle.

Sam wondered whether the magnetic field that radiated from

the ancient Chamber of Knowledge might have played a part in it as well.

He and Goddard stepped into the main building.

Its façade had a portico with six Ionic columns, which were flanked by two bell towers. Being a rotunda, the church had a circular plan with walls about thirty feet thick to support its massive dome, which had a diameter of one hundred and twenty-two feet.

The interior contained eight niches, including a deep apse with the main altar.

Sam and Goddard split up to search the interior, including the eight niches and deep apse.

A couple minutes later, Sam heard his name.

He turned to come face to face with Sandi Larson, the anthropologist who had taken the *Homo neanderthalensis* mask.

"Hi Sandi," Sam said. "How was your flight?"

"It was okay, thank you." Her eyes searched the massive dome wall above. "Find anything?"

"No, but Goddard's gone to talk to a priest about the previous church, built during the Renaissance, on which this cathedral was eventually built."

"Neat. Any guess what we're going to find here?" Sandi asked.

"I don't know. Goddard thinks this is an ancient vault, which stores all human knowledge."

Sandi cocked her eyebrow. "That's a bit fanciful, don't you think?"

"Sure, but everything about this is unique. Whatever it is, it's valuable if people are willing to kill to get to it."

Sandi opened her mouth to speak, and then stopped.

Goddard approached at the pace of a much younger man.

Sam glanced at him. He wore a broad smile. "What did you find out?"

"The Basilica of the Assumption of our Lady doesn't have a crypt…"

Sam sighed. "But?"

"The previous church did." Goddard grinned. "What's more, the priest offered to take us down into the hidden passageway, which descends all the way down to the historic site."

CHAPTER FORTY-EIGHT

RHYSE VAUGHN TURNED HIS BACK so that they didn't see him.
A woman next to him complained that he was blocking her view of the altar. He silently mouthed an apology, and took a step out of her way, following Andrew Goddard as he moved toward the east wing of the cathedral. Rhyse didn't have to work hard to conceal himself. The horde of tourist faces did that job for him.

He watched as Reilly, Goddard, and a woman he didn't know disappeared through a vaulted doorway at the end of the sanctuary, along with a priest.

Rhyse waited a moment and tried the door.

It was locked. He cursed under his breath and tried to push the door hard. It wouldn't budge at all. He glanced around the room, trying to think of a way to break through. There was nothing. The door was made of Spanish hardwood. It would take him half an hour with a good axe to break through.

No matter, he would just have to wait until they returned.

It wasn't a long wait. The priest returned, but without his guests. Rhyse set his jaw. Feeling his heart in his throat and blood pounding in the back of his ears, he set the timer of the bomb to thirty minutes and pressed start.

The priest looked at him, startled by his penetrating gaze. "May I help you, my son?"

Rhyse withdrew his silenced handgun and aimed it at the priest. "Yes, father. Forgive me for I am about to sin."

CHAPTER FORTY-NINE

The Obsidian Vault

S AM, GODDARD, AND LARSON ENTERED the 16th century crypt.

The first floor housed large marble vaults, where bygone kings and noblemen and women were once buried. Similar to the Hypogeum of Ħal-Saflieni, there were multiple superimposed levels hewn into the soft globigerina limestone. Dismissing the relatively modern marble vaults of the first level of the crypt, the three of them continued down the descending passageways interconnected through a labyrinthine series of steps, lintels and doorways.

The levels spiraled downward.

On the second level, the tombs seemed less ostentatious, made from cheap sandstone, and by the time they reached the third and fourth level, the place looked like ordinary catacombs, with bones strewn around every nook and chamber.

Sam swept the beam of his flashlight down every opening, across the rows of human bones, and then stopped.

At the end of the very last passageway, stood a single tomb

made from obsidian. It looked identical to the one that he'd found inside the Third Temple—an Egyptian pyramid buried in the Kalahari Desert, where the Master Builders once ruled as Gods.

"That's it!" he said, his voice soft, no more than a whisper.

Goddard made an audible exhale. "You're sure?"

"Almost certain. You heard our tour guide back at the Hypogeum of Ħal-Saflieni. She said Malta had no natural obsidian. That means this doesn't belong here."

Larson said, "It could have been shipped in from overseas."

"Sure," Sam admitted. "But if it was, I can tell you now it would have been placed at the first tier of the crypt, alongside the rest of the noble class, not at the bottom of the catacombs."

"He's right," Goddard said. "Let's remove the lid."

Sam shined his flashlight around the room. "That might be easier said than done. That lid must weigh three or four hundred pounds."

Goddard stepped into the next chamber, flicking the beam of his flashlight around the chiseled room.

He returned a minute later with an iron prybar.

Sam glanced at the tool. It was roughly six feet long, with a tapered end that could be slid underneath the lid, and used to pry the tomb's lid open. It was perfect. In Sam's gut, he felt fear churn. The tool was an anachronism. That meant that someone else had brought it down more recently.

The question remained, did that person already have two or more masks?

He swallowed down the fear, clamping the idea out of his mind, so that he could concentrate on what needed doing.

Goddard inserted the sharp end of the prybar into the tiny gap between the lid and the main vault of the tomb, and pushed down hard.

Nothing happened.

He tried again. "I might need a little help here."

Sam and Larson moved in closer. Gripping the prybar with each of their hands they heaved again, but nothing moved.

They tried again.

And again.

And on their fourth attempt the seal broke.

Goddard shimmied the device further into the gap beneath the lid. It was large enough now that the prybar could be fully inserted.

"On the count of three," Sam said. "One, two, three!"

All three of them heaved down on the bar. The lid shifted, sliding to the side, crashing off the edge.

They stepped forward and reverently peered inside.

Where seven hollowed out faces stared back at them.

CHAPTER FIFTY

S AM TOOK A DEEP BREATH.

The myth was real. The Master Builders knew about the seven species of the genus, *Homo* and had manipulated their natural path of evolution.

Sam looked at the delicate imprints of seven ancient faces, carved perfectly within the glossy obsidian as black as the night's sky.

He turned to Goddard. "Do you think we just place the masks into their respective molds?"

"That seems like a reasonable idea."

Goddard removed his mask from his backpack, lowering it to the mold that matched. It was a perfect fit. He stepped back, and the mask glowed red until it became sealed in the obsidian as though no mask shaped mold had ever existed.

Sam felt his heart beat faster. "It fits."

"Now mine." Larson carefully removed her mask, inserting it into the mold that matched. It glowed blue after a couple minutes, and then fused with the rest of the obsidian. "Now what?"

Sam turned to Goddard, who shrugged and said, "Beats me."

All three of them held their breaths.

A full minute passed.

The silence was broken by the sound of ancient machinery, like masonry cogs grinding on each other, working beneath the obsidian tomb.

"Get back," Sam warned, and they all took a few paces backward.

When the sound stopped, the entire tomb slid forward, revealing an open passage that descended into an obsidian tunnel.

Sam shined his flashlight inside.

The light disappeared down the ancient stairway.

Goddard said, "Who wants to go first?"

Sam opened his mouth to offer.

And Larson beat him to it. "Ladies first. I'll go."

Sam followed behind closely. The obsidian passageway was narrow. He had to turn his shoulders sideways to squeeze through. It was a tight fit, but didn't get any smaller as they descended. After travelling at least a couple hundred feet downward, the passageway opened up into a single obsidian chamber.

At the center of the vault stood an obsidian pedestal with pictographs of all seven ancient faces etched in the glossy stone surrounding it, above which were sealed crystal vials. Each one contained some sort of liquid.

A text, written in the ancient script of the Master Builders lined the top of the pedestal.

Goddard stared at the writings. "Any idea what it says?"

Sam studied it for a moment. He had spent more than a decade studying the ancient language, a code some still believed was nothing more than a giant hoax.

He then read it out loud.

"Herein remains the remnants of seven ancient viruses."

Sam felt fear rise in this throat.

"Consume the liquid contents of the vial that matches your species. Each vial contains the Phoenix Plague and the antidote for the matching species. Only one person from each victorious species needs to consume the liquid. The Phoenix Plague will spread rapidly to all who come into contact, destroying all other human sub-species. From the fire of destruction, the remaining immune species shall rise to unimaginable power and rule the Earth."

"Good God!" Larson yelled. "What have we done?"

Goddard shook his head. "No, no... you misunderstand it. We need to drink from the ancient vial."

The muscles in Sam's face tightened, twisting into abject horror. "You can't be serious, Goddard!"

"Why not?" Goddard's face looked hurt. "You heard what the ancient script said, from the fire of destruction like a Phoenix we'll rise as the top of the evolutionary ladder, filled with unlimited power."

Sam's voice was vitriolic. "What right do we have to destroy other species?"

"What other species?" Goddard replied. "*Homo sapiens* are the last species of human on Earth. We're not killing anyone. We're just empowering our species with enlightenment!"

"No, you can't. It's too dangerous!" Sam protested.

Goddard's lips twisted into a smile filled with greed. "That's where you're wrong. Failing to release the Phoenix Plague will condemn us all."

He reached for the vial that matched the mask that he placed in the obsidian tomb.

Sam said, "Stop!"

"I'm sorry Sam; I'm doing this for us — for all of humanity..."

Larson shouted, "You can't, that's not the *Homo sapiens* vial!"

Goddard's gray, bushy eyebrows narrowed. "Are you sure? It certainly looks like Homo sapiens to me?"

"No. It's Homo neanderthalensis!"

Goddard examined the vial and laughed. "So it is. My mistake. But you see, I am *Homo neanderthalensis*. And so are roughly two percent of the world's population. Which means if I drink this vial, I'll release the Phoenix Plague, killing ninety-eight percent of people on Earth. With the world's current resources, *Homo neanderthalensis* shall rise as kings on Earth."

"You're mad!" Sam said, moving toward him.

Goddard withdrew a handgun and aimed it directly at Sam. "I'm afraid this isn't going to play out well for you, Mr. Reilly."

Sam's eyes narrowed. "You had a gun hidden at the Xagħra Megalithic temple! I knew you had retrieved something!"

Goddard spread his hands. "Guilty as charged. I was worried you might need some persuading. Now stand over there."

Sam raised his hands in supplication. "Don't do anything stupid."

"I don't intend to."

With his right hand holding the handgun on Sam and Larson, Goddard reached for the vial in his left hand, lifting it up to his lips.

Sam dived toward him.

The obsidian chamber was filled with the echoes of gunfire.

Sam hit the ground hard. Opposite him, Andrew Goddard lay still with three bullet wounds to his chest, which no longer rose or fell with breathing.

The vial was empty.

At the entrance to the chamber stood the man who had attacked them in Venice. The same man who had tried to kill Sandi Larson back at the disused gold mine in the Monarch Mountains of Colorado.

He held a silenced Glock at Sam and Larson. "You'd better

head up those stairs unless you want to join your friend."

Sam asked, "Why?"

The stranger said, "A bomb's about to explode in a little less than ten minutes."

Sam looked at the suitcase. "You're from the Defense Department! Someone knew the truth, didn't they? That's why someone at the Pentagon authorized the Phoenix Sanction."

"We needed to be certain we had the right person."

"What are you, CIA? FBI?"

"I'm a ghost. And I was never here." His eyes locked with Sam's. "I suggest the two of you weren't either."

Sam said, "How do I know that you're not going to steal the vials of another species? How do I know you're *Homo sapiens*?"

"You don't. But I have the gun and the bomb." The man placed the suitcase next to the pedestal. "And I'm leaving now whether you come with me or not."

Sam nodded. "That's good enough for me."

All three of them raced toward the surface.

Back outside the Basilica of the Assumption of our Lady they mingled into the crowd. Below them, they felt the faint rumble of a large explosion.

Beside them, a woman said, "I think we just had a small earthquake."

Sam agreed. "It felt like it, didn't it?"

He turned to thank the ghost for saving their lives, but already the man had disappeared into the crowd.

Sandi looked vacantly toward the horizon, her mind far away. "Now what?"

Sam said, "I know a great beach near here that serves wonderful cocktails. Care to join me?"

Epilogue

The 8th Continent, Pacific Ocean

Three weeks later, Sam and Tom returned to the 8th Continent.

It was submerged in the South Pacific, a few hundred miles east of New Zealand, but once formed part of Australia. The entire place looked like it belonged in a Jules Verne novel. To access it, they needed to navigate a submersible into a large underground grotto. It used to be a volcanic atoll, but in the past fifty years had sunk to a depth of eighty feet. The entire beach, protected by a strange obsidian dome, remained filled with air.

Sam walked passed the well preserved remains of Amelia Earhart's Electra.

They descended the thousand plus stairs that led to the underground world.

Once there, the ceiling in the vault was so high that it could only be seen at the edges of the wall and not in the middle. A warm ray of sun shone down from above on the entire subterranean habitat, making him feel like he'd just stepped out into the great expanse of an ancient savannah. Giant trees and shrubs were covered with fruits he had never seen before, filling his nostrils with rich fragrances.

His eyes swept the near-mythical environment with wonder. It was impossible to tell where the place began and where it finished. It might have been a small country in its own right. Thick rainforests, including giant gum trees, more than a hundred feet tall, filled the area. There were massive open plains of grass, a freshwater river that split the ancient world in two, with multiple smaller tributaries and streams that ran off from it.

An 80-foot waterfall raged somewhere to the east, sending a fine mist down upon the valley. The sound of birds chirping echoed throughout. Ancient megafauna, oversized mammals, drank by the bank of the river.

Sam and Tom headed into the jungle, toward a clearing near the river some three miles away. The sun was setting and they spotted a single light coming from a nearby cottage. It seemed rudimentary, more of the sort of place where Robinson Crusoe might have lived. A single-roomed log hut, with a waterwheel fed by the nearby stream, and a garden of remarkable flowers.

A woman was whistling a gentle tune inside.

Sam glanced at Tom, who shrugged.

He knocked on the door.

A woman opened it.

She was roughly 5 feet 8 inches, with a lanky build and proportionate features. Her blonde hair, which was cut short, blew in the light breeze. She wore an impish smile, revealing a nice set of even white teeth, with a distinctive gap in the middle of her upper front incisors.

Sam took in a deep breath. "Amelia Earhart?"

The woman laughed. It was the sort of laugh Sam could get used to hearing. Full of joy and filled with life.

"No. She was my grandmother."

THE END

Want more?

Join my email list and get a FREE and EXCLUSIVE Sam Reilly story that's not available anywhere else!

Join here ~ www.bit.ly/ChristopherCartwright

Printed in Great Britain
by Amazon

21776101R00173